The Clemente Ball

Nora,
Happy reading!

Brian Croasmun

Brian Croasmun

Printed in the United States of America.

First Edition, 2019

ISBN: 978-1-7331651-0-5 (print)

ISBN:978-1-7331651-1-2 (ebook)

Author's website: www.briancroasmun.com

Edited by Jolene Perry of Cookie Lynn Publishing Services

Cover design by Chase Croasmun

This book is dedicated to Sherry, Chase and Davianne. This has been a family project from the beginning and your support for me has been unwavering. Words cannot express how grateful I am for having you three in my life.

CHAPTER ONE

Lucas looked in toward the catcher and stared a moment before bringing his arms up with his hands together. He raised his left leg, drew his right arm back, and let loose with a mighty throw.

Whack!

"Lucas! Watch what you're doing out there! I don't want that door dented any more than it already is."

"Sorry, Mom."

High, ball one. If the Pittsburgh Pirates were going to win the 1971 World Series, Lucas was going to have to settle down and get the ball in the strike zone.

He retrieved the tennis ball and resumed his position on the pitcher's mound at the end of the sidewalk. A couple of quick flicks of the ball into his worn baseball mitt, and he was ready to go again.

He reared back and heaved another throw that hit flush on the rounded corner of the cement front porch step. A line drive came right back to Lucas that he snagged with ease.

"Ugh!"

He was aiming for the flat front of the third step. The ball would then come back as a grounder straight up the sidewalk, just like the ground ball that Jackie Hernandez fielded to get the last out and win the World Series. Lucas had the play burned in his memory. He would recreate it himself. He wasn't going to give up now. He was Steve Blass, the pitcher, and Blass never gave up when he was on the mound.

Usually, Lucas would be Roberto Clemente and try to hit the rounded edge of the second step sending the ball high into the air and hopefully into the street for a home run. He'd already accomplished this feat earlier to match the homer Clemente hit in the game, but now he needed to get this last out so he could celebrate.

Whack!

No yelling this time, but his mom's face appeared in the window of the storm door. He saw a wry little smile cross her face as she stepped back from the screen. He removed his hand from his mitt as he picked up the ball to rub it down while he waited for her to retreat into the living room.

Another windup, another pitch, another ball popped high into the air.

He grabbed the black bill of his gold Pirates cap and removed it so he could wipe the sweat from his forehead with the side of his mitt. He'd hit that step a thousand times before just playing around, but now the target seemed impossible. He took a couple of deep breaths, yanked his cap back on his sandy blond head, and set up for one last try.

The dirty green tennis ball left his hand smoothly on its way to the steps and once again made contact.

Bonk!

2

There it was! The ball came bouncing straight up the sidewalk toward Lucas. He scooped it as the voice of TV announcer, Curt Gowdy, rang through his head.

"There's a drive up the middle. Hernandez at the back of the bag."

Lucas turned to throw the ball to the imaginary first baseman, also on the front steps. The throw hit squarely on the rounded edge and shot a line drive right back to him. His sudden accuracy froze him a moment before he recalled the rest of the announcement.

"He's got him! Hernandez with the grab. Blass has pitched the Pirates to the world championship!"

Lucas ran into the grass and jumped in the air with his glove and hand raised exactly how Blass had done. The celebration continued for a few seconds until Lucas heard a familiar voice.

"What are you doing, man?"

His next-door neighbor, Mike, had just shut the woodgrain tailgate to his family's blue station wagon, snapping Lucas back to reality.

"Just playing around. Throwing the ball against the steps," answered Lucas.

"Looks like you must have won the game," said Mike as he tucked his t-shirt back into his blue jeans.

"Yeah." Lucas chuckled nervously. "I've been trying to hit that one step for a while now and finally got it."

"Really? You're acting like you won the World Series." Mike laughed at his joke.

"Did I? Oh, yeah." Lucas forced another chuckle, also much less enthusiastic.

He started to tell Mike what he was doing but stopped himself. Mike wouldn't make a big deal of this. He was a year older than Lucas, but he often came over to play ping-pong and invited Lucas over to watch football. Lucas wasn't that big of a Steelers fan, but he did enjoy watching Mike's dad when he watched football, especially when they lost. There was something about a grown man yelling at the TV that Lucas found humorous. Mike ended up breaking the brief moment of awkward silence himself.

"It looks like someone is moving into that big house on the corner of Hanson Street. A girl was standing in the yard I didn't recognize. Might be someone new at school this year," explained Mike.

"Did you see any other kids?"

"Nah, just the girl. That was probably the biggest moving truck I've ever seen. Huge. I guess you'd need lots of stuff to fill up that house. Want to ride over and take a look?"

"Sure. Let me go tell my mom."

"Lucas opened the door, stuck his head inside, and yelled, "Hey, Mom! I'm gonna ride bikes with Mike for a while."

"Make sure you're back here in time for dinner. I'm making pork chops and fried potatoes."

No way would he miss his favorite meal.

The boys hopped on their ten-speeds and headed down 7th Avenue for the short trip to Hanson Street.

They made the ride in no time and started squeaking their brakes to watch the giant truck unload.

Desks, dressers, and tables were being handled with care as a line of men carried them into the house.

"Do you guys live around here?"

A girl's voice rang out behind them and Lucas stiffened his shoulders while Mike snapped his head sideways. Lucas turned his head slowly in the direction of the sound.

"Uh, yeah," answered Mike. "We live a couple of blocks over. I guess you're the one moving in?"

"Yep. My name is Jessica Snider, and I'm going to be in the sixth grade." She flipped her long brown hair off her shoulders.

"I'm Mike Cunningham, and this is Lucas Billman. I'm in the seventh grade, but he's going to be in the sixth grade with you."

"Will we go to the same school?"

"Yeah," Lucas chimed in. "We'll all be in the same one. If you look down that way, you can almost see it from here."

Lucas pointed in the direction of the building, even though there wasn't anything visible resembling a school in sight. However, it was in that direction, so he wasn't lying. He couldn't think of anything else to say.

Jessica pointed at Lucas's head. "I see you have a Pirates hat on. Do you like the Pirates?"

Lucas gave Jessica a puzzled look. He looked straight up toward his hat, then pulled it off and pretended to wipe his forehead while he snuck a peak at which hat he was wearing.

"Uh, yeah."

"I went to see them play last year with my parents. It was during the World Series. They let me skip school that day."

Lucas saw a couple of the World Series games on TV, but some of them he had to hear on the radio during school. He was lucky his teacher let them do their assignments while the game was on in the back of the classroom. He'd run home as fast as he could after school to see how the game ended, since the bell had rung before it was over.

Jessica stared at Lucas and blinked her eyes a couple of times. Lucas didn't know what to say since she hadn't asked him a question. He looked at the ground before responding. "Well, I've got to get home for dinner." Lucas turned his bike around and began pedaling up the street with Mike right behind.

"Gee whiz, why'd you take off so fast?"

"I don't know. I didn't know what else to say to her."

"I thought you'd talk about the Pirates. You always talk about the Pirates. I try to talk to you about the Steelers and you talk about the Pirates. I say, it's lovely weather out here today, and you talk about the Pirates."

"I've never heard you use the word lovely before." Lucas rolled his eyes.

"It's new. I'm starting today." They both laughed. "By the way, I think my family is going to a game next week. My dad only likes football, but he came home the other day and said he wants to go to at least one baseball game. Probably be the only game he goes to. You guys ever going to this year?"

"I don't know. My mom keeps saying not to bug my dad about it until they get stuff fixed at work. I guess the drivers might go on strike or something, and she says not to bother asking him stuff right now."

"I can't believe you haven't gone to a game this summer since you've been going on and on about the World Series last year. I'd think if anyone deserves to go to a Pirates game, it would be you." Mike was unintentionally rubbing a little salt in the wound.

Lucas couldn't answer right away. He wanted Mike to stop talking about going to a game since he didn't know if they'd even go this year. He took a deep breath before saying anything. "Mom says someday it will settle down and we'll go. I don't know. We'll see."

Lucas closed his eyes and slowed his breathing down before letting out a sigh. He paused, swallowed hard and turned his head, so Mike didn't see him wipe his eyes as they continued to pedal back home.

Lucas came home the next afternoon in plenty of time for dinner. He grabbed the newspaper and checked to make sure it said, Thursday, August 10, 1972 on the top before he turned it straight to the sports page to read about the Pirate game from last night. If he wasn't going to see them live, he could at least follow them through the paper. He sat down in his dad's recliner and began to read the article when his dad came walking through the door. Lucas started to get up.

"Sit down, sit down. I don't always have to sit there. It just feels good on my sore back." His dad placed his hand on his lower back and stretched back and forth a couple of times.

Lucas wanted to get up and let his dad rest his back, but he didn't want to disobey a simple command. Plus, this chair was comfortable. A quick compromise popped into his mind.

"Want the paper, Dad? It's already opened to the sports page."

His dad gave a small grin, and the corner of his mouth turned up a bit underneath his bushy mustache. It was the first time his dad had come home in a good mood for a while. Lucas started to smile back, and he wasn't yet sure why they were happy. His dad sat his hat on the end table and began to reach into his shirt pocket.

"I'll get the paper in a minute. I've got something to show you first."

Lucas knew his father didn't have a flair for the dramatic. The long pause that followed his announcement was unexpected. Lucas began to squirm in his seat.

"How would you like to go to the Pirate game this Saturday?" He flashed a pair of tickets that he handed to Lucas. "We had a delivery down by the stadium today, and I had one of the guys get us a couple of tickets. I assume you'll want to go."

Lucas couldn't stop the smile spreading across his face. He nodded his head as he handed the tickets back to his dad, who promptly took them and tapped him on the head.

"I hope we get to see Clemente play."

"I think you're going to get to see plenty of Clemente on Saturday," his dad replied.

"What do you mean by that?" Lucas asked.

His dad's bushy moustache rose as he stared at Lucas revealing the corners of his mouth curling up. He nodded his head as he tilted it sideways.

"You'll see."

Lucas sat in the front seat of the station wagon while his dad started up the engine and put it into gear. He drove the car out of the driveway and soon they were on the highway headed to the game.

"I bought our tickets in the lower section down the right field foul line," explained his dad.

"Why are we sitting there? We always sit in the outfield," asked Lucas.

"The outfield section sits too high above the fence. I wanted us to get a better view of Clemente in right field, so I got us closer."

Lucas fidgeted in his seat, constantly looking out the window of the car. He stretched his neck to see if they were getting close to the stadium.

"Can I get my own bag of peanuts today, Dad? I think I can eat a whole bag myself."

"A whole bag by yourself? Don't get sick or your mother will yell at both of us."

"I promise. I'll take my time and eat them during the whole game and not all at once."

"Don't get too wrapped up eating peanuts and forget to pay attention. A ball could come flying right into the section where we're sitting." There was a serious tone to his dad's words, but Lucas chuckled to himself with the thought of a ball hitting his peanut bag, watching the shells and nuts go flying in every direction, then reaching in and pulling out a baseball. After taking a peek at his dad's expression, Lucas kept the story to himself.

As they entered the stadium, the sun burst out from behind a cloud and lit up the large baseball field. Lucas stared left and right and up and down as they followed the usher to their seats. He had been here at least a half-dozen times but was still taken in by the enormity of the place compared to the ball field he played on at the city park. They settled into their seats, and Lucas's eyes widened again when he grasped how close they were to the field. The artificial turf told him this was a place where professionals played.

"We've never been this close before, have we?"

"I always like the outfield seats because they're cheaper. I thought we would treat ourselves to good seats, for once."

"Look, Dad! That's Willie Stargell right there. Wait, there's Bill Mazeroski! Can I yell to them like some of the other kids?"

"Be polite, address them properly, and they might respond."

"Mr. Stargell! Mr. Mazerkoski! I mean, Mr. Maskeroski! No." Lucas was flustered.

"Try, plain old Maz," suggested his dad.

"Hey, Maz!"

Lucas thought he turned toward them and winked, but he wasn't sure if it was toward him or the other fifteen kids trying to pronounce Mazeroski. It might not have even been a wink. He was trying to get a good look at Mazeroski's face when he was interrupted by more players walking past.

"Manny, Manny, I mean Mr. Sanguillen!" Lucas yelled and waved as Manny Sanguillen waved toward all the kids. He turned around in time for a ball to smack inside his catcher's mitt. The kids went quiet when they saw the throw came from none other than Roberto Clemente.

Lucas waived to his dad then pointed toward the dugout near where Clemente was catching the return throw from Sanguillen. Lucas couldn't get anywhere close through the thick crowd.

He tried standing on his tip-toes, but he couldn't see any better. He pushed the seat down and stepped on it, raising his height considerably.

"Careful. I don't want you falling," said his dad.

"Can you hear how that ball cracks the mitt when Clemente throws it, Dad? He's barely even trying."

"You never know, Lucas. You might be able to throw hard like that someday."

The game began with the Cincinnati Reds getting two runners on base with one out, setting up the most fantastic play Lucas had ever witnessed. A short fly ball floated into right field, and Clemente came sprinting up and toward the foul line. Lucas, his dad, and most of the fans around them stood up as they saw Clemente dive head first and snatch the ball inches from the ground, just in front of their seats. The runner at second tagged up and took off running for third. Clemente popped up off the ground, quickly drew the ball back and fired a rifle shot toward third base. The throw beat the runner by at least ten feet, quickly recording the final out. The Pirates began running off the field as the runner kneeled at third base gazing back out to right field, once, twice and then a third time before shaking his head and trotting over to get his glove from a teammate.

"Wha..." was all Lucas could manage to come out of his mouth.

His dad leaned in close to Lucas. "See why we got the better seats?"

Clemente was scheduled to bat third, and his turn came after two quick outs. He strolled to the batter's box, gave his neck a couple of twists and settled into his batting stance. The pitch came in with high speed, and after a loud crack, was sent out the same way. The ball went screaming into foul territory toward the right-field seats. Lucas squeezed his bag of peanuts as he tried to estimate the flight trajectory. He turned and ducked his head as the nearest crowd began to scramble for position to catch the ball. After a couple of seconds, everyone settled down, and Lucas straightened up. He could hear a few of the fans around him let out sighs of relief as a small round of applause erupted from the fans behind them. Lucas unfolded himself. His dad had a strange smile across his face and his rough, strong hands clenched a baseball. Lucas stared at his dad's hands, then up to his smiling face, then back to his hands again. Lucas also began to smile.

12

"Sign that guy up," yelled one of the fans in the upper rows.

"What a catch!" yelled a younger man who slapped his dad on the back a couple of times.

Lucas smiled even more as he continued to stare at his dad who gave a quick nod to the fans behind them, then returned to his seat along with the rest of the row. He handed the ball to Lucas revealing large red patches on the palms of both hands. Lucas's eyes were drawn to the ball now in his possession. He turned it over in his fingers until he could read the National League Baseball stamp as his dad flexed the fingers on both of his hands. Another loud crack came from home plate as Clemente flew out to deep left field and Lucas didn't even look up to see it. He was only concerned with the ball he held on his lap.

"How did you catch this thing, Dad?" Lucas asked in awe.

"I didn't duck away like you did, Lucas," he answered as he held back a chuckle. "I told you to pay attention when we sit in this section. I wasn't lying. The old man still has a little skill left in these hands, don't you think? I wish the feeling would come back now." His dad winked and gave a quick laugh as he shook his hands back and forth in front of him.

The rest of the afternoon was a whirlwind. The momentum went back and forth the whole game, as one great play after another unfolded in front of him. Even the easiest of plays made Lucas's heart race and his pulse jump.

Clemente had made another strong throw from the outfield, but this time the runner didn't try to get to the next base. "Look at that throw! He was too chicken to run. He knew Clemente would have nailed him." Lucas laughed.

"The coach held the runner at third because that catch made two outs," explained his dad. "You see, they don't want to risk missing out on an opportunity to score. If there was only one out, they might take a chance, since there would still be the other runner on base."

"Oh, I see," answered Lucas, even though he wasn't sure he did. He remembered his baseball coach teaching them something about never making the last out at third or home plate, but it didn't make much sense. He was sure of one thing; the throw was better than the one in the first inning making it the best throw Lucas had ever witnessed. The game of baseball had never been more alive, and Lucas was still holding a piece of the action right in his hands.

The Pirates held on to win the game 5-4, even though the Reds had the tying run at third base when they made the last out. The excitement kept the whole crowd in their seats until the end, so the fans packed the concourses when they got up to leave. Lucas felt the crunch of the peanut shells under his feet when he started down the aisle making sure to check his grip on the prized baseball.

"Hey, kid, how'd you get a ball?" asked one happy fan walking beside them.

"My dad caught it," beamed Lucas as he turned toward his dad and smiled. "Clemente hit it!"

14

"You're going to want to hold onto to that one," the fan responded.

"I think we're going back to the World Series this year," an older gentleman said to the woman walking with him. She merely nodded and smiled.

They both made their way back to the station wagon for the trip home. The slow traffic leaving the stadium gave them time to reflect on the day.

"Did you think anyone could throw a ball like that, Lucas?" Those may have been the best throws I've ever seen, and I'm closing in on fifty years old."

"Me, too," Lucas agreed.

"What are we going to do with this ball when we get home?" Lucas wondered out loud.

"I've got an idea," answered his dad.

They pulled into the driveway, and Lucas hopped out of the car and headed straight through the back door into the kitchen where his mom stood at the stove stirring over a large pot. The smell of noodle soup wafted across the room and caused Lucas to sniff the air. He walked over to the stove and looked into the pot with a smile before turning to his mom.

"You should have seen the catch Dad made! He snatched this thing right out of the air with his bare hands. Clemente hit it!" Lucas held out the baseball. He didn't mention ducking for cover and never seeing Dad catch the ball. His dad stood inside the doorway with his small grin barely pulling up the corner of his mouth. "There were people in the stands cheering for him," Lucas continued.

"Sounds like you two had fun today," replied his mom.

Lucas was interrupted by his dad who pointed toward the garage. "Bring the ball and come on."

He held the door open for Lucas, then followed him into the garage. He shuffled around the car and headed for the back of the garage where Lucas was waiting.

Dad grabbed a two-by-four and headed for the band saw. He made a quick measurement and cut a square piece off the end. Next, he took it over to his drill press, put in a wide bit and drilled a hole larger than a quarter down the middle. He then pulled out a piece of sandpaper, handed it and the block of wood to Lucas, and asked him to sand it smooth. While Lucas was sanding, his dad got into the corner cabinet and pulled out a can of dark walnut stain and a brush. He watched Lucas rub the sandpaper all over the wood and pointed out one corner needing a little more attention. He finally took the wood back from Lucas, blew the sawdust off with a couple of sharp breaths, and sat it on the work table with the stain and the brush.

"I want you to give this a nice coat of stain, Lucas. Maybe two, if it dries quickly enough. Pull the brush all the way across nice and slow, so the stain evens out." He showed Lucas a sample stroke of the brush, then handed it to him to finish. "Be careful not to get it on your hands; it doesn't come off easily. We'll leave it to sit out here and dry overnight."

After dinner, Lucas had returned from taking his bath to find his father holding the ball in the living room.

His dad turned the ball in his hands like Lucas had at the game. Lucas couldn't help but notice his dad's signature grin as he stared at the ball. He looked up toward Lucas and put the ball down on the coffee table.

"You'd better head to bed before your mother yells at both of us," his dad joked. "We'll check the stand in the morning before we leave for church."

Lucas woke up Sunday morning to find his parents at the kitchen table sipping on cups of coffee. Lucas wiped both of his eyes with the back of his hands and gave a couple of long blinks until everything was in focus. The stain should be dry by now.

"Want me to get the stand?" asked Lucas. His dad nodded toward the garage door. Lucas came back a moment later with a smooth, stained piece of wood.

His dad took the wood from Lucas's hand and inspected it carefully. He walked into the living room and picked up the baseball from the coffee table. Lucas followed him. His dad held the wood flat in his left hand and carefully placed the baseball on top of the hole in the middle. He wiggled his hand ever so slightly to test if the ball would stay nestled in the hole. He turned to show the completed project to Lucas.

"I know exactly where I think we should put it. Follow me." Dad shuffled over to the door leading to the basement. They both trotted down the stairs to the family TV room. He took the ball over to the shelf above the television, moved a picture frame toward the middle, and placed the ball near the end, then stepped back to check it over. Lucas noticed the stain matched the wood paneling on the wall, so the stand disappeared into the background, making the ball appear to be floating. He continued to gaze at the ball until everything else went out of focus.

"Whad'ya think?" asked his dad.

"I think this is a great spot for it. I don't think anything can happen to it down here."

His dad retreated back up the stairs while Lucas stayed a moment to look at the ball. He pictured himself someday throwing a baseball as young kids circled the field to watch. They fought for position in order to get a better look. He imagined the crack of the bat as the ball went flying in the air. He began running the bases, feeling the wind in his hair. The roar of the crowd filled his ears as he stopped on the base to take it all in.

"Someday," Lucas said out loud to himself. "Someday."

CHAPTER TWO

Lucas came up the basement steps followed closely by Mike. Lucas's mom turned around quickly from the kitchen sink when the basement door closed behind them.

"That was a quick game of ping-pong," his mom said.

"We weren't playing ping-pong," answered Lucas, "something else."

"He caught that with his bare hands?" asked Mike.

"Yep. Reached up over his head and snatched it clean," Lucas answered. He assumed that was how it went since he didn't see it when he ducked.

"I don't think my dad could catch a wiffle ball if I threw it to him underhand. Remember that time he tried to play out back with us? He kept striking out, then tripped trying to catch a fly ball and all of the change fell out of his pants pocket." Lucas snickered and nodded his head.

"Yea, I remember. Well, anyway, after he catches the ball, half the section starts clapping for him. The other half was kinda mad when they didn't catch it."

"How close did you come to catching it?" asked Mike.

Lucas paused and pretended to think by twisting his mouth and raising his eyebrows. He shook his head.

"I didn't have any chance at all."

Mike had turned his head and missed Lucas's sigh of relief. His answer was accurate without being a lie.

"I still bet it was pretty cool to be right there when it happened," replied Mike.

"Yep." Lucas was thinking fast on what to say next, but nothing was coming to mind. He started to open his mouth and confess how he ducked away behind the seat when the ball came.

"I better get home. Wish I could stay and play football out back, but Mom says we're leaving for grandma's, and if I'm not looking out that back window of the station wagon when we pull out, I should wave bye because they won't be turning back around to get me." Mike laughed as he walked out the door. Lucas let out another sigh of relief for not having to reveal how a baseball player like him was afraid of a ball.

Lucas was studying the sports page of the newspaper and sitting in his dad's recliner waiting to hear the car pull into the driveway. He popped up as soon as he heard the car door shut and waited until his dad came through the door.

"I've got free tickets to a Pirates' game," his dad said.

"Did you know how close Clemente is to getting three-thousand hits?"

"Wait. What?"

His dad opened his hand, and Lucas recognized the stop signal while they each smiled and stared at the other. His dad reached into his pocket and pulled out two rectangular pieces of cardstock with the Pirates' logo on one end and September 30, 1972, printed right on the top. "We got these at work for advertising in the Pirates' program this year. I'm not sure how good the seats are, but we need to go to another game this year," his dad explained. "Now, what was this about three-thousand hits?"

Lucas had always tried to remember the lessons his dad taught him about baseball history, even if the details often became fuzzy shortly after hearing them. Hank Aaron and Willie Mays were famous names he could recall, but he wasn't sure why he remembered them. Two years before, in the summer of 1970, both famous baseball icons achieved their three-thousandth career base hit in Major League Baseball. Lucas couldn't grasp how significant the number three-thousand was at the time. He remembered how his dad had called him over to the kitchen table and shown him the newspaper article after both men had reached the milestone. However, he didn't believe it had even crossed his mind again until now.

It was Lucas's turn to show his dad an interesting newspaper article. Lucas pointed to the article titled, "Clemente Closing in on Monumental Hit." Lucas stared toward the ceiling for a moment and went silent. It was the same expression he would sometimes make when doing his homework right before he came up with the answer.

"Can he do it, Dad? Can he get to three-thousand hits before the end of the season?" asked Lucas.

"How many does he need?" asked his Dad.

"He needs thirty-five more. Is that too many? He might already have it if he didn't get sick a few weeks ago. At least, that's what the paper says. How hard is it to get thirty-five hits? How many hits did I get this year?"

"I'd say you had about fifteen, so you'll need two-thousand-nine-hundred and eighty-five."

"Is that all?"

"You only played thirteen or fourteen games."

"I should get twice that many next year, don't you think? I'll be one of the older kids."

"As long as you're willing to work at it. Now let's get back to Clemente. He missed over a month, so it's going to be close. Let's hope he can keep his strength up." Now his dad was staring at the ceiling. "He must hope he doesn't go into any bad slump, doesn't get hurt or run into any rainouts. He needs to get one hit every game, and every few games get a second. On average, of course."

"What's the date for those tickets?" asked Lucas as he raised an eyebrow and raised his voice a little higher.

"September thirtieth. The last Saturday of the month. The last Saturday of the regular season. And yes, you're probably thinking what I'm thinking. We could get lucky and be there for the big hit. We could also miss it by a day or two. He also might not get there this season. Let's wait and see what happens."

"I'll try, but I can't help wondering if we're going to see it," said Lucas.

"We'll just keep track the next few weeks and see. Promise me you won't get too disappointed if we don't get to see it happen. It's a longshot, really." He spread his hands a few feet apart for emphasis.

"I'll try not to be disappointed." He opened his hand and nodded his head.

The promise was easier said than kept. Over the next couple of weeks, Lucas was giving daily reports on Clemente's progress toward the prestigious number.

"Look here, Dad." Lucas had just opened the paper from mid-September. "Three more hits last night. How many does that make this week?"

His dad pretended to count on his fingers. "I think we counted ten yesterday, so that makes thirteen."

"Shoot! He's going to get there too fast!" Lucas made a fist.

"Make up your mind, Lucas. Do you want him to get to three-thousand or not?"

"Yes, but, you know, I'd like to see it."

His dad opened his hand toward Lucas. "If it happens, it'll happen. I warned you about this."

"I know, I know." Lucas nodded his head and sighed.

"Maybe we could go to a game before we go to the one we have the tickets for."

"Sure. Go pack a suitcase and we'll catch the next flight to New York City."

"Really?"

His dad stared a moment before Lucas started shaking his head.

"Alright, I'll quit worrying."

The month was dwindling, and so was the number of hits Clemente needed to reach the historic mark. Hit number two-thousand-nine-hundred and ninety-nine came on a Thursday night in Philadelphia. Lucas saw the news in the paper the next morning and worried he could have slept through the big moment. Again, Lucas had a conflicting thought about Clemente. He was only one hit away, and Lucas had tickets for the game on Saturday. There was only one problem. The Pirates played on Friday night against the New York Mets.

Dad tuned the game in on the radio in the basement like he had done numerous times throughout the summer. Often, he would turn the sound low, then turn on the television or work on some household project, keeping tabs on the score from time to time. Earlier in the season he would take the radio outside while it was still daylight and listen from the front porch. Similarly, Lucas would be playing ping-pong with Mike or out with other kids from the neighborhood during the game. Tonight, they both sat down in the basement with the radio.

Lucas suddenly came to a strange realization. Were they cheering for Clemente to break the record tonight or not? It seemed odd to want Clemente not to get the big hit. What if this caused a slump lasting through the end of the season? Would he feel responsible for Clemente's misfortune? What if he got the historic hit tonight when they were less than twenty-four hours from being there to witness it? Would he be happy for his dad's hero or upset for both missing it? He wondered how his father felt, but his dad wasn't saying much.

There was already a runner on base when Clemente made his first plate appearance. The crack of the bat came loud and clear through the radio speaker as Lucas and his father both sucked in a quick breath. The ball went off the glove of the second baseman and into right field allowing both runners to be safe. Lucas and his dad listened carefully while the announcer made the official call. "It will be ruled an error on the second baseman. No base hit." They glanced at each other, still not sure what their reaction should be.

The game moved quickly through the evening since neither team could score a run through the first eight innings. Clemente wasn't having a great night. He struck out in the fourth inning and hit a weak grounder back to the pitcher in the sixth. The Mets found a way to score a run in the top of the ninth, so the Pirates would have one last chance to tie or win the game, and Clemente was going to be the first batter. He wasted no time in taking a whack at the first pitch he saw, sending it screaming into right field. The excitement swelled through the static on the radio. "Fly ball to right field. Staub goes back aaaaaaand makes the catch near the wall."

Lucas and his dad looked at each other and both shrugged their shoulders. Lucas cracked a smile. Clemente was going to have to wait until tomorrow to get his big hit and now Lucas was going to be there if it happened.

He didn't wait for the last two outs before heading to bed. His dad announced the Pirates lost 1-0 as he finished brushing his teeth. Now, it was a matter of being able to turn off his mind so he could fall asleep. He tossed and turned a few times trying to settle down for the night. He ended up getting out of bed and going to the bathroom to get a drink of water to break up the monotony. He wasn't sure how much longer it took to fall asleep once he returned to bed, but it didn't seem long before his mother informed him there were pancakes ready in the kitchen.

Lucas sat down to the table and smiled at the big stack of pancakes.

"Did Linda or Laura come home this weekend?" Lucas asked about his sisters away at college.

"No, they didn't," Mom answered.

Lucas didn't need to ask anything else. He speared as many pancakes as he could with his fork and carefully lifted them onto his plate. A large pat of butter and a long pour from the syrup bottle had Lucas ready to eat his fill before the big day. His dad came in and sat down at the table already dressed. He sipped his coffee cup while he scanned the morning paper.

"We're going to leave a little sooner than we usually do, in case there's traffic," said Dad.

There was always traffic, and they still made it to the games on time. Lucas figured this was his dad's way of saying he was excited about going to the game. Now that he thought about it, he couldn't remember his father ever using the word excited unless he was telling Lucas not to be.

Lucas filled his belly with breakfast, put his dishes in the sink, and headed to his room to get dressed for the game. Roberto Clemente was going to get his three-thousandth hit today and Lucas was going to be there to see it. Then he overheard his mom in the hallway.

"What happens if Clemente doesn't get a hit today?"

Brian Croasmun

CHAPTER THREE

"What if we catch another ball hit by Clemente today? What if we catch his three-thousandth hit?" asked Lucas.

"First of all, the only way we could catch the big hit is if it was a home run, and we're not sitting in the outfield. Second, I'm not sure where this section is where we're sitting. I think it might be behind home plate, but we've never sat in these seats before. I don't know if a foul ball comes there often or not. I guess we'll see when we get there."

The parking lot wasn't even half-full when they parked the station wagon. Lucas stepped out, zipped up his jacket, and looked around the lot.

"Where is everybody? We saw so much traffic, I thought this place would be packed."

"I bet a lot of them went over to the university to watch the Pitt football game."

"Who wants to watch football when Clemente is about to get his three-thousandth hit?"

"I know, son. Some people just go crazy over football. Let's go find these seats."

They made the long walk through the main gate then halfway around the stadium until they reached the side printed on their tickets. Lucas walked beside his dad as they made the turn inside the main concourse. They climbed the first ramp and found the sign with their section on it with an up arrow beside the number.

They navigated a U-turn and began the walk up the next ramp that went overhead of the ramp they just climbed. They found another sign with their section on it and Lucas's shoulders slumped as he saw the arrow beside the number was still pointing up.

"We're not there yet?" asked a panting Lucas.

"Oh, keep going. This little walk isn't going to kill you," answered his dad.

They changed directions again and ascended the next ramp to see the sign for their section didn't have an up arrow this time. The arrow was a right angle pointing to the left.

"What does that arrow mean?" asked Lucas.

"We go up one more ramp and turn left."

Lucas took in a deep breath, then started the final push up the ramps. They turned left into the open concourse which was much quieter than the one at the bottom. Their footsteps echoed as they moved down the almost empty hallway until they reached their section.

They stepped through the doorway, and Lucas caught a view of the stadium that he had never seen before. He stared at the field as his dad checked over the tickets.

"Look how high up we are. This stadium is huge," whispered Lucas to himself.

Lucas started to squint toward the outfield, then turned to his dad.

"There he is. There's Clemente! This is going to be so cool."

"It will be in a few minutes. Look what row we're on," said his dad as he pointed to the word ROW JJ on the tickets.

Lucas chugged up the steps with renewed vigor. He looked over his shoulder to see his dad was still a few rows behind trying to catch up. He turned back around and started to bolt back up the steps until he reached the end of the alphabet and the beginning of the double letter rows. His breathing was heavy, but he was antsy to get to his seat.

They were finally near the highest rows in the entire stadium when they heard laughter from a few of the others in their seats.

"You got free tickets for buying advertising too, huh? You've got the right seats. We didn't know the stadium went this high, either." The rest of the row burst out in another laugh. People began introducing themselves quickly, and Lucas couldn't remember a single name. He'd never sat in a group where so many people were talking and laughing together at the stadium. This was going to be a fun afternoon, even if there was no way possible a player could hit a foul ball up here.

Game time neared, and the stadium was still not half full. Lucas had been anticipating this day for a couple of weeks, and it turned out to be the magical opportunity he had hoped for, yet there were thousands of empty seats in this cavernous stadium. Was this a special day or not?

The crowd may have been smaller than Lucas expected, but the noise they created early was noticeable. Some games took a few innings or at least an exciting play to get the crowd started, but today they were already making their voices heard. One section near them had started a "Cle-men-te" chant before the game's first pitch. A few joined in from a different section, but it died out when the first batter for the Mets came to bat.

The Mets had one baserunner reach on a walk, but the other three were put out easily on some weak ground balls to start the game. The intensity began to rise when Chuck Goggin hit a single to get on base for the Pirates. However, both runners were quickly put out when Rennie Stennett hit a sharp ground ball that the Mets turned into two outs on a double play. It didn't matter. The crowd was here to watch the next batter break into an exclusive club.

Roberto Clemente strolled to the plate, and the crowd rose in unison. They watched the familiar gyrations he made with his head and neck, and his confident stride as he approached the batter's box. A couple of wiggles of the bat and he was ready. The first pitch came screaming by him for strike one. Clemente wasn't going to let the next one go. He swung with all his might and this time made contact. It wasn't solid enough, and the ball went flying backward over the backstop netting. It continued to climb heading right for Lucas and the free ticket crowd. Lucas raised in his seat when he saw he was right in the line of flight. Gravity pulled it back down about twenty feet short of the lowest row of the upper deck, far below them.

The disappointment of learning no ball would be reaching them today was nothing compared to the frustration to come on the next pitch. A looping curveball bent toward the plate, and Clemente couldn't resist. He hadn't counted on the ball dropping so low he would have needed a canoe paddle to reach it. A swing and a miss for strike three. "He struck out last night, too. The season is going to end tomorrow, and he might not get the big hit," said Lucas.

"There will be lots of chances, yet. Quit worrying," answered his dad.

The next two innings crawled along as there was little action. The crowd was restless for something big, and their cheering had faded out. Nothing else mattered until Clemente got another turn to bat.

Finally, the bottom of the fourth inning arrived, and Clemente was due to bat first. On cue, everyone rose to their feet, and a roar began to swell through the crowd. For the first time today, Lucas's breath came out short and quick. He couldn't stand still. Clemente strode to the batter's box, grabbed some dirt to rub in his hands, then used his bat to knock some dirt out of his cleats.

"Come on, Roberto, come on," shouted Lucas as he pumped his fist up and down.

Lucas looked at his dad who replied with a nod and a slight smile.

Clemente wasted no time. The first pitch came buzzing in and was sent right back out into the outfield between the left and center fielders. The ball hit the turf and bounced up against the fence. Clemente used his familiar stride to fly around first and ease into second base. Hit number three-thousand had arrived.

Lucas let out a scream as he punched both fists into the air. The crowd responded with shouts of appreciation.

Lucas watched as the infielder gave the ball to the umpire, who in turn, handed the ball to Clemente. Clemente then tossed the ball to the first base coach for safekeeping. Lucas would have loved to have that ball on a stand in the basement. He scanned the giant scoreboard in centerfield and noticed:

ROBERTO IS NOW ONE
OF 11 PLAYERS IN MAJOR
LEAGUE HISTORY TO GET
3000 OR MORE HITS

The hit ignited a rally by the Pirates as they scored three runs in the inning to take the lead. Clemente was taken out of the game to rest because the Pirates were going to be in the playoffs soon and Clemente had been under a great deal of pressure to get this monumental hit. They scored two more runs in the sixth inning to take a 5-0 lead. His dad told Lucas they had seen what they came to see; the tickets were free, so he wanted to head home and avoid the worst part of the traffic. Lucas couldn't disagree. He was anxious to get back to the baseball in the basement.

Lucas replayed the hit over and over again in his mind on the drive home. The second they pulled into the driveway, he ran into the house.

"Mom, Mom, he did it! We saw the three-thousandth hit!"

"You must have been good luck for him, Lucas. It was a good thing you showed up."

She gave him a quick hug, and he giggled under his breath. His mom always found a way to give him credit for something somebody else had done.

Lucas hung up his jacket and went down the basement stairs. He slowed down once he left the bottom step, then proceeded quietly to the shelf above the TV. He picked up the Clemente Ball and held it in his hands. The same excitement shot through his body as it had on the day they brought the ball home. Once again, he started daydreaming about cheering fans, running the bases, and stopping to hear the roaring crowd. He pictured himself standing on the base while he looked around about to win a big game. He never wanted this feeling to end.

Brian Croasmun

CHAPTER FOUR

"What's this?" Mike picked up the folded newspaper from the small bookshelf in Lucas's room.

"Newspaper. You've seen one before, haven't you?" chuckled Lucas.

"Funny. This one is over a month old. I'd think a bunch of new stuff's happened since this came out. Might want to think about getting another one."

"I forgot it was even there."

Lucas knew it was there because it was right where he left it the day after the Pirates lost the last playoff game to the Cincinnati Reds on a wild pitch.

"Look, it's open to that game the Pirates lost at the end of the year," said Mike.

Lucas knew exactly what page it was on.

"That was the craziest way to lose a game. Man, that stunk," continued Mike.

"Yep. If the Pirates had won that game, I would have gone to the World Series," answered Lucas.

"No, way."

"I'm not kidding. My dad said you never know when it might be your last chance to see something like that, and he wasn't going to miss it again like last year.

He said he was going to find us tickets, and I could have skipped school and everything, but it didn't happen."

"Oh, yeah, right. That stinks."

"Uh, yeah. It was only going to be the coolest thing to ever happen in my life. I was pretty ticked off about it." Lucas gritted his teeth and made a fist. Mike chuckled at first, then pulled back when he saw Lucas's reaction.

"I guess you're right. I'd be ticked off, too," answered Mike. "I better get going. Got to get going to my grandma's for dinner so I can watch my grandpa overeat, fall asleep in the chair, and see if his dentures stay in or hit the floor like last time."

Mike laughed harder than Lucas as he headed toward the door. Lucas turned around and put the newspaper back in the same spot on his shelf.

"You guys are coming over when you get back, aren't you?" asked Lucas.

"Of course. We can't break in the new year anywhere else but in your basement."

A short while later Uncle Roy drove his pickup truck into the driveway with Grandma in the front seat. Uncle Roy came into the house carrying a basket with a couple of dish towels draped across the top while Grandma had brought some kind of pie.

"I stole this from Little Red Riding Hood on the way over here and thought we could have it for dinner," laughed Uncle Roy as Lucas opened the front door. Lucas then took the pie from Grandma and brought it to the table while she took off her coat.

"Everything smells so good in here," Grandma said.

"Not everything," joked Uncle Roy as he grabbed Lucas's wrist and raised his arm, exposing his armpit. Lucas rolled his eyes and gave Uncle Roy a small smack in the stomach with the back of his hand.

"Lucas why don't you and Uncle Roy go downstairs and tell everyone that people will be arriving shortly?" asked his mom.

"All right."

Lucas's sister Linda was home from college and sat on the couch with her new boyfriend while his sister, Laura, visiting during the holidays, sat cross-legged in the recliner.

Lucas stiffened up when he was about to speak as he saw Linda's boyfriend was holding the Clemente Ball. Lucas had shown the ball and told the story before, but he didn't like a teenage boy whose name he didn't even know manhandling it.

"Why didn't you throw that ball back, Lucas, so they could keep using it in the game?" asked Linda. Her boyfriend looked at her and furrowed his eyebrows. "Why are you keeping it?"

Linda's boyfriend kept making throwing motions with the ball, and Lucas was getting more nervous. Lucas had forgotten why he came downstairs, but he wanted to get the ball away from the boy before something terrible happened.

"Want to see it, Uncle Roy?" asked Lucas.

"Sure, let me take a look at it," answered Uncle Roy.

The boyfriend tossed the ball underhand, and Uncle Roy caught it cleanly.

"So, Clemente hit it, and your dad caught it. That's the story you want everyone to believe. Did you see him catch it yourself?" Uncle Roy rubbed his chin.

Lucas couldn't answer right away. He wasn't ready to admit he got scared and ducked away. Uncle Roy would be the first one to laugh at him.

"My guess is, he picked it up off the ground after the old lady who caught it dropped it into her popcorn. Is that what happened?" Uncle Roy burst out laughing at his joke.

Lucas reached out his hand, and Uncle Roy placed the ball softly in his palm. Lucas carefully put the ball back on the stand and made sure the National League stamp was facing the front before he and Uncle Roy went back up the stairs.

A couple of families from the neighborhood, and one from his dad's work, were joining them in a little New Year's Eve party. Mike and his family from next door were coming, too.

Marvin and his wife showed up a little bit later. Lucas wasn't sure precisely what Marvin did at Donovan Trucking, but he knew it was something in the office part of the building. His one son was already out of school and had been a good baseball player in town. Donovan Trucking sponsored a team in the local youth baseball league, so Marvin always acted like a pseudo owner. He came by some of the games and would put whatever team trophy they might win in the office window. He was well liked in the community because he supported the kids without butting in or taking over and was lots of fun to be around. Marvin exchanged pleasantries with everyone in the room and found himself standing in front of Lucas and his dad. He stared directly at Lucas.

"So, tell me, Lucas, did this guy catch a ball hit by Clemente or were those bruises on his hands from clapping so hard when he goes square dancing?" Marvin let out a laugh and smacked his dad on the shoulder with the back of his hand. Lucas laughed at the thought of his dad square dancing, gave a quick "follow me" wave, and headed back down the basement steps. Marvin obediently came, accompanied by his dad.

Lucas went straight for the ball and handed it to Marvin. He examined it intently and even gave an exaggerated nod to Dan, who had remained on the bottom step.

"It was a great catch. Everybody in the stands cheered for him and made a big deal of it."

Marvin flipped the ball back to Lucas before retreating up the steps with his dad. "Don't lose it, kid. Hear me? Did you ever think about taking it to one of those events the team holds and asking Clemente to sign it?"

"Really? You think he'd sign it?"

"I can't promise he would, but they have players make appearances around the area to meet fans to get them interested before the season."

"That would be so cool. Thanks for the idea."

Lucas couldn't remember enjoying one of these get-togethers more. Mike and a few other kids his age were down in the basement having a ping-pong tournament while most of the adults were upstairs in the kitchen and living room. There was food everywhere, and a couple of different card games between the rooms.

Lucas had lost a close game to Mike and went upstairs to refill the basement party's chip bowl.

"Catch any more foul balls down there, kid?"

"I heard Clemente might show up tonight. Says he wants his ball back."

"He'll have to fight me for it," answered Lucas as the adults burst out in laughter.

Sometime later in the evening, everyone gathered down in the basement to watch a new show, *Dick Clark's New Year's Rockin' Eve*, he was hosting from New York City where the big ball was going to drop in Times Square. They were finally going to be able to watch something live they had only heard about in the news or read in the papers.

Lucas was over by the ping-pong table and could no longer see the television. He could hear the music playing, but the noise in the basement had become so loud he couldn't tell what the song was.

"Here it goes," came a man's voice from the front of the group.

"Ten, nine, eight, seven,"

Lucas tried to stretch his neck to see the small screen.

"Six, five, four,"

He decided to quit straining to see and join in.

"THREE, TWO, ONE! HAPPY NEW YEAR!"

"HAAAPPPPYYYY NEW YEAR!" screamed Lucas.

The adults began hugging and kissing on each other, so Lucas backed up behind the ping-pong table until they all settled down.

The crowd started breaking apart as a few made their way back up the stairs. A couple of women stayed downstairs and started throwing all of the half-eaten snacks, empty chip bags, and drink cans, into a garbage bag. They had the room cleared in a couple of minutes.

Everyone had gone back upstairs, and Lucas shut off the television and all the lights before joining them. Most of the crowd had finished cleaning up the upstairs and started making their way out the door to their cars.

Lucas put on his pajamas and got himself ready for bed. His mom stopped him in the hallway on his way to brush his teeth.

"You were quite the celebrity with everyone tonight talking about that Clemente Ball." His mom smiled and raised her eyebrows as she started to take the pins out of her hair.

"They all wanted to hear about it, I guess. Do you think we could go to something and get Clemente to sign the ball?"

"Starting tomorrow we'll look around and see if he is ever going to be around here."

"And I'll make sure to get you there," said his dad, who appeared in the hallway.

"Thanks. I can't wait."

Lucas brushed his teeth and went to bed. He was tired from a great party but the excitement of getting the great Roberto Clemente to sign his baseball wouldn't let his mind rest. What would he say to Clemente? Would he tell him how popular this ball has made him? He finally nodded off right in the middle of practicing how he would greet Clemente when he met him.

Lucas woke up well after his usual time. He laid still in the quiet of his bed while replaying some of the moments from last night through his mind. The sun had become bright, and he wondered why someone hadn't told him to get up, or he would be fixing his breakfast. He got up, shuffled out the door, down the hall and into an empty kitchen. The coffee pot was warm, and there were some toast crumbs on a plate on the table, so he knew his parents were awake. The basement door was half-opened, and he could hear his parents whispering.

"Are they sure?" asked his mom.

"I think they're pretty sure, but they can't confirm anything yet. I guess there is still some hope until they have some real evidence."

Lucas had eased himself into the doorway, and saw his dad sitting in the chair in the basement holding a baseball and his mother sitting on the edge of her seat at the end of the couch. She noticed Lucas and waved for him to come down. She slid over and patted the couch cushion signaling Lucas to take a seat. Instinctively, she began lightly rubbing his back. Something must have happened, but he couldn't understand why his dad was holding the Clemente Ball and turning it so nervously in his hands. Dad finally cleared his throat and began to speak.

"Lucas, there have been some reports this morning that Roberto Clemente was killed in a plane crash last night." He paused as Lucas straightened up in his spot. "He was on a plane carrying earthquake relief supplies from Puerto Rico to Nicaragua. It took off last evening, and it disappeared shortly after takeoff. One report said the plane radioed about coming back, but there has been nothing since, and it has been more than twelve hours. They should have landed somewhere by now."

Lucas sat quietly for a moment taking it all in. Maybe they got lost and landed somewhere else. Perhaps they landed and got busy unloading supplies and forgot to radio back. Lucas had never flown on a plane before, so he had no idea what could have happened. It was hard imagining a tragedy that didn't seem real.

"But I was going to get his autograph," Lucas said. "I was going to get the Clemente Ball signed by Clemente."

"I'm sorry, Lucas," replied his mom.

"You said they don't know where he is? Maybe he's still alive. Maybe they have it all wrong."

His mom exhaled out of her nose and put her index finger across her lips. "Yeah, but there doesn't seem to be any way..."

"Well, if they don't know anything, they can't say he's dead. I won't believe it until I hear it for sure. Can I get some breakfast?"

His mom showed a puzzled expression over Lucas's head. His dad shrugged his shoulders and nodded his head upward toward the basement stairs. "Why don't we go upstairs and get some toast and cereal," suggested his mom. She patted Lucas on the back as they got up and ascended toward the kitchen.

Lucas made quick work of the cereal and toast his mom had set in front of him. His sisters must have still been in bed as his father remained in the basement. "What's Dad still doing in the basement?"

"I think the news this morning surprised him. Why don't you run down there and see what else he is up to?"

Lucas wiped his mouth one last time, pushed his chair under the table, and walked to the basement steps. His dad was sitting in the same spot, still holding the Clemente Ball. He slowly crept downstairs hitting both feet on every step so that he wouldn't surprise his dad.

Once Lucas had reached the bottom step, his dad looked up. He slid back in his chair and patted the armrest as he nodded for Lucas to join him. Lucas sat on the big armrest because the days of squeezing in the chair with his dad were long gone. He put an arm around Lucas to secure his seat while still holding the ball in the other hand. An uncomfortable silence filled the basement. After a few seconds, he squeezed the baseball and started to speak.

"I suppose you're wondering why I'm so upset about hearing this bad news when it's somebody we don't know or are even related to."

Lucas sat still not knowing what to do.

"As you know, I lost my father before you were born. He was planning to retire in a few years and wanted to spend more time going to baseball games, particularly to watch this new kid, Clemente, and watch him grow as a player. We saw him play together once — just one time. I've always kept an eye on his career and made it my business to learn as much about him as I could. He was more than a great ball player. He's been a great human being. Your grandfather would have liked him."

"How do you mean?" asked Lucas in a soft voice.

"I know you've heard stories about how Jackie Robinson became the first black baseball player and all the hardships he had to endure, right?"

"Sure, I've heard some."

"Well, Robinson knew how poorly they would treat him. He had dealt with racism his whole life and was ready to stand up to it, no matter how bad it was and believe me, it was bad. Clemente, on the other hand, had no idea people were going to be like they were. He hadn't grown up with the same kind of bigotry in Puerto Rico. He didn't know he would have separate hotels or restaurants. He didn't know there would be out-of-control fans. He showed up and became a great ballplayer in spite of them. He became a great friend and teammate. I can't imagine what those guys are feeling like right now. You see, he was the kind of player and person I would want my son to grow up and follow. This country has changed a lot lately, and it's because of guys like him. When you finally asked me to take you to a game to watch him play..." He paused and took a few deep breaths.

Lucas was focused on his dad's face. He could feel the seriousness in his dad's voice, and he was hanging on every word.

"For some reason, when this ball started zooming our way, there was no way I was going to let it get by, no matter how much it hurt my hands. Boy, did it hurt."

Dad took his hand holding the ball and turned it over as if he was about to drop the ball. Lucas recognized the sign and put out both of his palms up so his father could deposit the ball in his grip. The ball fell softly, and Lucas felt a sense of warmth he didn't understand. His dad pinched his thumb and a finger at the top of his nose at the corners of his eyes and let out a sigh.

"Understand now why we brought the ball home and put it in a stand? This is our memory together, and nothing can ever take it away from us."

Lucas looked at the ball resting in his hands. He had never met his grandfather, so it was hard to feel sad about him, and he had only seen Clemente playing baseball. He knew he was feeling something, but he couldn't grasp the emotion coming from his dad, or himself.

He got off the armrest, walked over to the shelf, and returned the ball to its stand. He wanted to get out of the basement as fast as he could because he didn't know what he should do if his dad started to cry.

CHAPTER FIVE

Lucas and Mike drug their sleds and inner tubes on to the corner of Mike's yard. Mike started to peel off to the left toward his garage. Lucas continued across the grass.

"Incoming," yelled Mike.

Lucas turned in time to see a large chunk of snow burst apart as it crashed into his back.

"What's this?" laughed Lucas. He reached down in the middle of where the snow landed to find a dirty tennis ball.

"It belongs to my dog. Look how much better I throw a real ball in the snow," chuckled Mike.

Lucas turned and threw the ball back at Mike who grabbed it in both hands.

"Go long," yelled Mike, his cheeks pink with cold.

Lucas bolted into his yard with the sled and inner tube chasing behind on a rope. Mike threw the dirty tennis ball high, Lucas snatched it right before it hit his toes.

"Clemente catches the ball and fires home," announced Lucas in his head as he pulled back and let the ball fly on a line to Mike, who again, caught it with both hands.

"Nice throw. Now, do it again," replied Mike as he hurled the ball back in Lucas's direction. The ball landed to his left, so Lucas shuffled over as if it was a groundball to Jackie Hernandez, scooped the ball out of the snow, and fired it straight to Mike.

"What are you doing, fielding grounders?"

"I guess. It seemed more like the thing to do with a tennis ball, rather than act like it's a football," Lucas answered.

Mike picked up his arm and prepared to throw. "Here, backhand this one."

Mike threw the ball to Lucas's right, and he pretended to pick up a harder ground ball when it stopped in the snow. He fired another throw straight to Mike.

"This is why they don't play baseball in the snow," said Mike.

"It would make it hard to let a grounder go between your legs," said Lucas. He chuckled at his own remark.

A large black car with a big inner tube sticking out of the trunk drove past, and a girl waved from the front seat.

"Isn't that Jessica? She was the one who had the giant tube. I don't think I've talked to her since that day she was moving in. I never see her at school," said Mike.

"Might be. I dunno," answered Lucas.

He knew it was Jessica. He didn't want someone asking him at school on Monday if he was out in the yard playing baseball in the snow with an old tennis ball. Sometimes the other kids don't understand when they only see a brief second of action.

"I better get going," Lucas said as he dropped his sled by the back porch and headed inside.

He peeled off a couple of layers of clothes and jackets to dry by the back door. Lucas could smell the pot of hot chocolate on the stove. He slipped into some warm, dry clothes and came back to the kitchen to find his mom waiting with a steaming mug. He went to the table to join his dad but there was nowhere to set his mug down because there were papers strewn all about. His dad grabbed a few and stacked them up creating a spot for Lucas.

"What's all this?" Lucas asked.

"Life insurance policies," answered his dad without raising his head.

Lucas went silent. He didn't know precisely how life insurance worked, but he did recall hearing the term tossed about by adults before, and it didn't sound interesting. He took a couple of loud sips trying to get some of the hot chocolate into his mouth without burning his tongue. His dad's face went stern as his mom slid a plate of cookies on the table.

"Do you have to eat those here?" he asked, then glared at Lucas.

"Why don't you grab a couple of cookies and run downstairs and watch TV?" Mom suggested.

Lucas watched his dad's moustache curl downward, then grabbed three cookies and his mug and headed for the basement door. He took another loud slurp at the top of the stairs trying to minimize the amount of liquid he could spill as he descended the steps. A couple of small splashes still ended up on the side of the mug.

He sat his cookies and hot chocolate down on the coffee table while he licked melted chocolate from his fingers. He turned on the television and settled down to watch a *Gilligan's Island* rerun.

About halfway through the show, his mom came down the stairs bringing some more chocolate chip cookies.

"Mmm, thanks, Mom," he said as he reached for the plate.

"You're welcome, sweetheart."

His mom sat down in the chair while Lucas remained stretched out on the couch. She sat and stared at Lucas. He adjusted his pillow a little and glanced to see if she was still staring.

"What was all the stuff about life insurance up there?" asked Lucas.

"Your dad has been doing a lot of thinking lately. Since Roberto Clemente died so young, it got him to thinking about what would happen to us if anything happened to him. He wants to make sure, you know, everything will be covered, that's all. He doesn't like to bother you kids with this kind of stuff. Life insurance is awful expensive, so we've been comparing different policies to learn what we can afford. Nothing you need to worry about."

"Is that why he's been acting so weird lately?" Lucas asked.

"What do you mean, honey?"

"I don't know." Lucas took another bite and stared at the screen rather than his mom. "He just seems like he's upset a lot, but he never says anything about it."

"He's been tired and a little stressed lately. I think he'll get to feeling better when this winter weather breaks soon. I heard it's supposed to warm up next week."

"I hope. I wonder why this bothers him more, now? He was sad when Clemente died, but he looks like he is taking it harder now instead of getting over it."

"I don't think he's thinking about Clemente as much as he is thinking about you, me, and your sisters. He wonders if he's done enough to prepare for the future," his mom replied.

"I wish I could make him feel better. What can I do?" He turned both palms upward.

"Maybe we can get him to have some fun soon. Keep your eyes open for something you guys could do together."

Lucas felt the unseasonably warm air as he went to the porch to get the Saturday morning paper and decided to see if there was anything interesting in the sports section. He was surprised to find an article "Pirates Head South for Cooler Temperatures." Spring training was starting, and Lucas was caught entirely off guard. The rest of the article talked about how the team was going to have to pull together and overcome the loss of Roberto Clemente in the offseason and who might be the players they use to replace him. Lucas hadn't thought much about it. He was sad Clemente died, but since it happened over the winter, he had never thought about someone having to take his place on the team.

The front door opened, and his dad stepped inside after running out to get milk. Lucas kept the paper open to the article as he got up to show it to him. His dad took a glance as he headed toward the recliner.

"Yeah, I heard about this. I guess it's been warmer in Pittsburgh this week than in Jacksonville, Florida."

Lucas went to the kitchen table to eat a bowl of cereal while his dad sat down, put down his coffee, and opened the front section of the morning paper. His dad's eyes scanned across the pages, occasionally stopping to take a small sip. Neither one of them spoke. His mom sat down with her coffee and broke the silence.

"It's supposed to be warm today but turn back to cold by Monday. Maybe you guys should get outside and enjoy it while you can. You never know when it will be this warm again. What do you want to do now the snow is gone, Lucas?"

Lucas scrunched up his face while he thought for a moment. His dad turned and stared at his mom out of the top of his eyes.

"Can we pass baseball?" Lucas asked. His dad tilted his head and thought a moment. "I might be able to pitch some this year, so it wouldn't hurt to start getting ready."

Lucas was going to enter his final season in the town's youth baseball league this year. The twelve-year-olds were the biggest, strongest, and most talented kids, and Lucas couldn't wait to join those ranks.

His dad looked at his mom for a moment, then returned to the paper. He let out a sigh behind the obituaries.

54

"I think it's a great idea, Lucas. Don't you think so? Might not be this nice for long," his mom interrupted. "Get out of this stuffy house and enjoy the warm air and sunshine."

His dad waited another moment before giving his answer. "Let's wait about an hour for it to warm up a little more before we head outside."

Lucas nodded in agreement. His mom snuck a nod and a smile toward Lucas, so he hoped getting outside to do some baseball activity might help improve his dad's mood.

He finished his cereal and put his dirty bowl into the sink before heading to his room to get dressed. He made sure to put on a long sleeve shirt so his mother wouldn't force him to wear a jacket, since a jacket made it so much harder to throw. He dug out his glove, his dad's old glove, and a ball from the closet, then sat down in the living room to wait.

Dad came out of his room a few minutes later wearing an old gray sweatshirt and a Donovan Trucking cap.

They went out to the front yard and separated by a few feet. Lucas made a few light tosses and started to step back. He made a few more tosses then moved back again where he usually stood when passing baseball with his dad. He made a few more throws, and it was becoming apparent he was getting the ball there harder and with less effort. After a few more throws, he stepped back some more. The throws were still coming easily to him while making a loud crack into his dad's glove.

His dad even stopped after a couple of catches and stared at his glove for a moment. "Do you know how hard you can throw the ball now, Lucas?"

"It does feel like it's going a lot faster than I remember."

His dad pulled off his cap and scratched his head while looking right at Lucas. Lucas thought he was about to say something new but had no idea what his dad was thinking.

"How would you like to learn how to throw a curveball, Lucas? If you can throw this hard, I bet you could get the hang of it."

"Um, sure. Sounds pretty cool." Lucas felt a small surge of excitement go through his chest.

He handed Lucas the ball and reached down to arrange his fingers.

"Lay your middle finger on the threads right here. Put your index finger beside it as lightly as you can while still controlling the ball.

"Feels a little funny to hold it this way."

"You'll get used to that when you start to master the pitch. Make sure you twist your wrist like this." He then twisted his hand for Lucas to see. "Don't twist your elbow because that is how you hurt your arm."

Lucas flipped the ball into his glove a few times to see how it worked.

"Let's try a few and see how it goes." His dad moved back and tapped his fist into his glove a couple of times. "I don't expect you to do it right away."

Lucas reared back and tried to work through the motion. His dad jumped to keep the ball from flying over his head. The next one bounced off the ground before his dad snatched it.

"I think I can get it if I do it again," Lucas said.

The ball left his hand and was heading straight for his dad, belt high. He snagged the ball with his glove and grinned at Lucas with wide eyes. "Lots of spin, but no curve, Lucas. I said you probably wouldn't get it right away."

It didn't matter. Lucas had a tired arm by now, and his dad had taken his hand from his glove and was flexing his fingers. Lucas had made his dad's hand hurt. He could already feel the throws in the games he'd play this season. He could tell how much stronger he'd be as he swung the bat and ran the bases, too.

"Thanks for passing with me, Dad."

"No, thank you for being a kid who will pass ball with his dad. Some of the guys at work never get to do this with their kids. I appreciate you letting me try to teach you some stuff."

"I like that you do teach me about baseball. I always feel like I understand what I'm doing and that makes it more fun." He flicked his wrist to mime the curveball, already knowing it might keep him up all night. "I'll figure out that curveball."

They went back inside where Lucas took the gloves and the ball to put back in the closet. Lucas had never been this excited about playing baseball before, and he still had a couple months of practice before they really got started. This was going to be his best year of baseball, yet.

Brian Croasmun

CHAPTER SIX

The unseasonably warm weather continued and gave Lucas an idea during lunch at school. He leaned forward on the lunch table. "Hey, do you guys want to head over to the field later to play a little baseball? The tryouts are coming up, and we could start getting ready?"

"When?" asked Timmy, one of the boys in Lucas's class.

"After school today. We can head over around four or four-thirty and have a couple of hours to hit and throw," answered Lucas.

"I'll come," said Jeff, a boy who had played on Lucas's team last year.

A few of the other heads nodded in agreement, and only a couple sounded like they weren't interested.

Jessica Snider peered up the table from her spot near the end. "Where is the baseball field around here?"

"Why do you want to know?" answered Lucas.

"Because I just moved here after baseball season and I don't know, that's why?"

Lucas felt a twinge of guilt for sounding snarky. "It's at the city park down past Main Street. The softball field is down there, too."

Lucas had not been around Jessica much this school year, but he did know she knew about the Pirates. She said she was sorry when the Pirates lost in the playoffs, but Lucas hadn't carried the conversation further.

Lucas couldn't wait to show off his new arm strength to the other boys. He hadn't mastered the curveball, or had the ball curve at all, for that matter, but he knew his arm was stronger than it had ever been.

Lucas approached the field on his bike with Mike by his side. Both had their baseball gloves on one side of the handlebars and a bat across the top. Timmy and Jeff were already standing on the infield.

"Look at all the puddles on the infield," Timmy said. "It's still wet from the rain we had yesterday."

Jeff pointed to the field as he pushed up the sleeves on his sweatshirt. "The outfield doesn't look bad in the grass. Let's go out there and see if we can do anything."

"Yea, maybe we can throw or something," replied Lucas. He wanted to throw more than anything.

The four of them paired up and started to make throws back and forth in the outfield. Even after a few throws, no one else joined them.

"I guess it's just the four of us," said Lucas as he raised his glove in preparation to catch Mike's throw.

"We wouldn't have room for too many more people if we're just staying out here in the grass, anyway," Mike responded, letting loose with another heave.

"I thought I saw Jessica ride by on her bike," said Jeff.

"She's probably checking out where the softball field is. I told her where to find it," answered Lucas.

Mitts cracked after each throw from the boys. They were backing up farther and farther, yet the ball continued to come in a straight line. It wasn't just Lucas throwing better.

"Do you guys feel like you're able to throw harder now?" Lucas asked the group as he adjusted the ball in his hands.

"I would think I would," answered Jeff. "We're all twelve now. We ought to be able to throw it better."

"I'm thirteen." Mike chuckled. "I could throw like that last year."

Lucas laughed because he knew Mike's favorite sport wasn't baseball, and he talked like he might not play anymore since he was moving up to the other league. Mike only came for something to do.

Lucas tried to put a little more into his throws to see if he could outdo the other guys, even if he were the only one who noticed. He wished he had the Clemente Ball with him. Somehow, he felt like he might be able to throw it harder than any other ball. But the slaps into Mike's glove from Lucas weren't any louder than the rest. Maybe he wouldn't have an advantage this year. He was throwing harder, but everyone else was, too. He'd really have to work hard before the tryouts if he wanted to be a top pick.

The boys stayed around for a little while longer throwing each other pop-ups and long fly balls, as best they could. They tried some other games like knocking a paper cup out of the fence with a throw and catching a ball from the air behind their backs. None of them made any sense, but Lucas was happy doing anything with baseball involved.

Lucas dropped one of the behind-the-back catches and heard a voice say, "Nice catch. Hope you do that when I hit one this year." Russ Ledbetter leaned against the fence while still on his bike.

"Yea, pop-ups are all you'll probably hit, anyway," said Lucas, keeping his eye on Mike and the ball.

Russ shook his head, then tossed his hair off of his forehead and began speeding away. Russ would always say stuff to make people mad and then leave. Lucas didn't turn around to watch him ride away.

"I'm heading home, guys." Mike picked up one foot at a time, inspecting them. His pants were soaked halfway to his knees. "My feet are soaked from all this wet grass."

"I'm coming, too," answered Lucas, his socks squishing in his shoes as he walked. "See you guys, later."

"See you at the tryouts. Maybe we'll get on the same team again this year," said Jeff.

"That would be cool," answered Lucas. He mumbled the rest of his reply to himself. "Because I'll probably be the last one picked."

Brian Croasmun

CHAPTER SEVEN

Lucas awoke on the day of the tryouts with his stomach in knots. TO be sure he was at his best, he slipped downstairs and flipped the Clemente Ball into his glove a few times for luck.

Many of the businesses in town sponsored teams in the league. They would often match the sponsors with the first players selected, if the business had a relative involved. If Lucas was one of the top choices, he would be playing for Donovan Trucking. His dad made it seem like it was no big deal if his company sponsored Lucas's team, but Lucas wanted it bad. He loved their blue and gray uniforms, and since his dad would be on the league board anyway, he wanted to represent his dad's team. Lucas had to be at his best.

His dad walked into the living and grabbed his car keys from the hook. "Let's get going, Lucas. I've got to get there and help organize these tryouts," his dad said.

Lucas flipped the Clemente Ball into his glove one last time, set it back on the stand, and left with his dad.

When they pulled into the parking lot, only a few other people had arrived. A couple of boys were hanging around the first base dugout, and Lucas joined his potential teammates while his dad went to the picnic table behind the bleachers. Lucas closed his eyes and slowed down his breathing before heading inside the dugout doorway as he tried to regain the confidence he felt that first time he threw with his dad.

The dugout started to fill up with boys coming for the tryouts. They were starting to bump into each other as some looked for a place to sit only to find the benches were full of boys. Timmy tried to squeeze into the doorway, then gave up and stood by the entrance.

"What's Jessica Snider doing over there?" asked Timmy as he stretched his head above the others.

"Where?" asked a voice in the crowd.

"In the other dugout," answered Timmy.

Lucas squeezed between a couple of players to come to the front of the dugout and look across the infield.

"Maybe she thinks there are softball tryouts today," said Timmy.

"They don't have softball tryouts. They barely get enough for two teams," answered Lucas. This ignited a murmur which traveled all through the dugout and back again. She could only be here for one thing. "I bet she's here to try out for baseball."

"Hey, Lucas, remember how she asked you where the field was? Well, here you go." Timmy adjusted his red baseball cap.

"I didn't think she wanted to play here. I figured she wanted to come to watch a game. I know she likes the Pirates." Lucas shrugged. "I thought she might like to see baseball games."

Lucas had never thought about a girl playing in the baseball league before. She was probably the only girl who'd ever mentioned baseball to him, aside from his mom. He didn't believe this was a stunt to stir up trouble because she had been a polite student this year. He knew she knew the rules, and he wondered now if she could play.

Lucas pushed his way out of the dugout so he could report to his dad who was sitting at the picnic table with a few coaches and men on the baseball league board.

"Do you see who is over there, Dad? It's Jessica Snider."

"We're aware of the situation, son." He put his hand on Lucas's shoulder. "We're talking about it right now."

"Does she know how to play baseball?" asked Lucas.

"I don't know, we haven't had the tryouts yet."

He gave Lucas a half-hearted wave, and Lucas plopped down on a picnic table a few feet away from where all the men were seated. Lucas scooted down to the end of the table closest to the men. Maybe they'd say something about Jessica, and he could understand what she was doing here.

"Seriously? We have a girl who wants to play baseball?" questioned one of the few men of the group Lucas didn't know.

Bill Quinn, the president of the town's baseball organization, spoke up. "Here's the situation, fellas. Yes, we have a girl who has signed up to play baseball. We have to consider this and decide what we are going to do."

Brian Croasmun

"Easy," said the man who had talked first, "tell her we have a softball league for girls her age. They're always looking for new players. They'd be glad to have her." A couple of the men agreed with a soft grunt or two.

"It's not that easy, Curtis," replied Bill. Lucas had a name to go with that person now.

"Her parents know we have softball and they still signed her up to play baseball. As it turns out, our league rules don't state baseball is boys only or softball is girls only."

"It shouldn't have to say it," answered Curtis. Lucas now remembered Curtis had his own tree trimming business he ran out of the back of his rusty old pickup. "Somebody go over and explain it to her parents. They'll understand."

Dean Sullivan, the brother-in-law of Bill and league vice-president, spoke up next. "No, they won't understand, and I'll tell you why. Any of you guys heard the name, Maria Pepe, lately?" The men all stared around the group waiting for someone to recall the name. "No? Hoboken, New Jersey? Still doesn't ring a bell? Then listen up, and I'll explain.

"Last year, this girl, Maria Pepe, tries out for the Little League Baseball team in Hoboken, New Jersey. These aren't tryouts like ours. You have to make it through two rounds of cuts and earn your place on the team. She gets talked into trying out by the people in her neighborhood and what do you know? She makes the team. She's also the best pitcher they had."

"Don't matter," interrupted Curtis, "tell her to play softball."

68

"Hold on a minute, Curtis, I'm not finished," snapped Dean as he gave a quick stare toward Curtis. "There were all kinds of complaints from some parents and coaches of other teams. Pretty soon the national Little League Baseball organization gets involved and says she has to quit, or they're going to pull the league's charter and drop their insurance. The Hoboken team asked her to quit, so she did."

"Exactly what I'm saying, let's get rid of her now."

"Shut up, Curtis, I've not made my point yet."

Lucas held his breath, not wanting to miss a word.

"The case went to court. The National Organization for Women are involved, and it appears it may be tied up in court a little while. A federal court could jump in and say a girl has as much right as a boy to play baseball. That's where it may be headed."

"How do you know all this, Dean?" questioned Curtis as his face went into a squint.

"Mr. and Mrs. Snider explained it all to us when they came to sign Jessica up, that's how. It turns out they are both attorneys and moved here to open the new regional branch of Keystone Legal Services around the corner from the courthouse. They weren't involved in the case, but they happen to be friends with one of the attorneys who is involved. They didn't threaten us with a lawsuit. They said their daughter only wanted to play baseball."

"Wouldn't they love a case to get some free advertising for their new office? Sue the league and get the whole town scared of you," warned Curtis.

Bill stepped back into the discussion. "We're not affiliated with the national Little League. We have our own youth league here in town. If some attorney hauled us to court, we'd be bankrupt. We only make enough money to cover our expenses from year to year. Anything like this would ruin us. What are we going to do, fellas? Any ideas?"

The group went silent for a moment. A couple of the men shuffled in their seats like they wanted to speak, but no words came. Lucas didn't understand the sudden silence. He didn't know which way this discussion was going to go and neither did these men, it appeared.

Finally, Lucas's dad broke the silence. "Is she any good?" More silence and lots of puzzled faces. "I mean, shouldn't we run her through the tryouts and find out? If she stinks and the boys are much better than her, she might want to switch to softball. If she is good, what's it going to hurt to let her play?" More awkward silence. "I'll take responsibility for her. I'll work with the coaches, I'll talk to the parents."

"Anyone have a problem with it?" asked Bill. "What about you, Curtis? You have any beef with that plan?"

Curtis thought for a moment, let out a sigh, and said, "Do what you want, I guess."

Lucas slipped back over to the boys in the dugout and hoped all the men hadn't noticed. The noise level had risen in the dugout, and some of the boys were wrestling around chasing each other in front of the doorway. The boys didn't see Lucas had returned.

Lucas was still processing the information from the meeting. His dad had offered to handle the situation with Jessica wanting to play baseball. Lucas wanted to be picked first so he could play for Donovan Trucking, the team his dad's company sponsored. Jessica was probably going to play for Donovan Trucking. Lucas answered himself out loud, "There is going to be a girl on my team." How was he going to explain this to the others?

Just as Lucas had melted back into the crowd of boys, he noticed his dad walking toward the dugout and gesturing for him to come over. "I'm going over to explain about letting Jessica try out to her parents, and I want to introduce you so they will know at least one other player."

His dad smiled as he spoke, and it helped Lucas relax his shoulders since he now felt better about the situation. It might not be so bad having a girl on the field when he goes out to play second base for Donovan Trucking, if he got to play for Donovan Trucking.

His dad found Mr. and Mrs. Snider standing together beside a tree behind the other dugout. He introduced himself and then Lucas. They all shook hands. Mr. Snider even gave a little tug at the bill of Lucas's baseball cap. His dad explained how they were going to give Jessica a chance to try out to find out if this is what they want to do, and if she stuck with baseball, she would play on the team his company sponsored.

"That's all she wanted," Mr. Snider replied, "a chance to play baseball. She's been playing with her older brothers for a while and has played softball before. She wanted to try to play baseball last year, but since we were in the process of opening the new law office and getting moved here, we talked her out of it. We thought getting a fresh start in a new town might be a better way to begin. I think you might be surprised when you watch her play."

Lucas went out to the field where they were organizing the boys, and Jessica, into small groups. The men chose which station each group would go to first. There would be fielding ground balls, catching fly balls, hitting, and base running. Not only was Jessica going to be on his team, but she was in his tryout group, too.

The first ground ball hit to Lucas bounced off his glove and trickled away. He had been so distracted by everything, he wasn't focused. He picked the ball up and flipped it back, then set up to receive another. He fielded it cleanly and made a crisp throw to the catcher. He started to play like the second baseman he knew he was. He had to get his mind on playing the game and away from the other distractions.

However, for every good ground ball scoop and strong throw Lucas made, Jessica wasn't far behind. She was outshining some of the other boys. He started to wonder if the coaches were going to notice any play he would make today because Jessica was taking so much of the attention. It wasn't until they switched to the fly ball station, he felt the coaches weren't staring at her intently. It was apparent she was able to play with the boys.

The tryout pace had slowed down in the fly ball station because they had to chase after a few of the bad throws before they could hit any more pop-ups. Lucas looked around to see if anyone was close. He decided he would try to talk to Jessica.

"So, what position do you hope to play?" he asked.

"Second base. There's not much to do out here in the outfield," she answered.

"We've got some kids in this league who can hit it out here now. A couple of these guys can hit it over the fence. I almost hit one last year. It bounced right in front of the fence."

"Yeah, but all the fun happens on the dirt. Even if you catch a fly ball out here, you only throw it back to the infield. I want to be where the action is, and second base is the one I play best," she finished.

Another fly ball came their way and ended the conversation abruptly. The coaches called for the players to go to the infield after the last fly ball. They explained how everyone would get a phone call this week letting them know what team they were on and when their first practice would be. The players gathered up their belongings and started to head home.

Lucas had looked forward to this day for months. Throwing with his dad early had given him more confidence in his own ability than he'd had in previous years, and now he might be playing for the team he wanted, but there was a girl who wanted to play his position-and she was good. Instead of going home excited about the upcoming, season, he went home disappointed and confused.

I will be the second-baseman for Donovan Trucking this year.

Brian Croasmun

CHAPTER EIGHT

"Hello?" Lucas's mom answered the phone. 'Yes, it is."
She turned to grab a piece of chalk to write on the little
board hanging on the wall. "Monday at 5:30? Yes, he
should be available. I'll tell him."

Lucas walked into the kitchen. "What was that call
about? Baseball?" He followed her as she walked across
the kitchen.

"Yes, you have practice on Monday at 5:30 at the
field."

"What team am I on? Did they say?"

"What team did you want to be on?" She failed at
hiding her grin. "Of course, you are going to be on
Donovan Trucking. Why wouldn't you be?"

"It means I was the top pick, that's why. They pick
your sponsor, so you play for the one where your family
works, if you have one. Oh, never mind. Dad will know
what I mean."

"You'll be the top player to me, Lucas. You
always are, sweetheart," said his mom.

"I know. Thanks." Lucas smiled, glad to end the
awkward part of the conversation. "I don't suppose they
mentioned any other teammates, did they?"

"No, they just told me you had practice. Don't forget, that girl is going to be on your team. Jessica, is it?"

"Yes, it's Jessica Snider. I'll have to find out who else is on my team at school tomorrow."

It didn't take long the next morning to find out who wasn't going to be on his team.

"Hey, Lucas. Are we going to have to pitch underhand this year or is your team the only one?" Ledbetter said from behind him.

"Shut up, Ledbetter," answered Lucas.

Lucas rolled his eyes and sighed to himself. Every time he responded it only got worse.

None of them said much when Jessica was around but weren't afraid to crack their jokes when she wasn't. There were even boys who didn't play baseball who decided to pile on, as well.

His dad's grand idea of trying to be the buffer between the naysayers and the supporters didn't take school into account. Lucas didn't want to run home and cry to his dad about what the kids were saying.

He knew there was nothing his dad could do to stop the things kids say away from other adults.

A couple of the teachers had heard about the situation and shared their opinions with Lucas, too. Ms. Miller, one of the P.E. teachers, said "I could have told you a long time ago Jessica could play ball, Lucas. She has a good arm and isn't afraid."

"Lucas, I've got some coaching advice for you," said Mr. Watson, the math teacher, "you can get to first base faster if you hold up your skirt when you run." A couple of other male teachers laughed but Lucas didn't. He slowly shook his head.

"We're just teasing with you, Lucas," said Mr. Watson.

Lucas still didn't think it was funny. However, most of the other teachers, male and female, wanted Lucas to tell his father they were glad he stood up for one of their students. This made him feel better, even if the situation was still a nuisance for him.

Finally, Lucas was at practice where he could get down to playing baseball rather than listen to everyone talk about it.

"Everyone giving you a hard time today, huh?" asked Timmy.

"Yea, pretty much. Did they say stuff to you?"

"Nobody knows I'm on this team yet, so I didn't hear anything," answered Timmy.

"Same here," said Jeff nearby. "It's going to change now. Isn't that Ledbetter on his bike over there spying on us?" He pointed toward the swing sets where a couple of boys watched them.

Lucas went back to trying to get his newly found strong arm noticed. He tried to crack the ball into Jeff's glove each time, but Jeff did nothing more than pull the ball out and throw it back. Timmy didn't say anything either while he threw beside them, but it was obvious to Lucas Timmy had the strongest arm on the team.

Earl Watkins was the head coach for Donovan Trucking, and he called for all the players to come to the infield. He was the vice-president of the bank and knew everyone in town but didn't know everything about baseball. He had some basic knowledge, but Lucas was hoping to get a coach who played college baseball or the one who owned the sporting goods store. Instead, he got Earl. The only guy who went to Earl for baseball advice was his next-door neighbor and accountant, Howard Ford, who would now be his assistant coach. It was tough to be too upset about them since they were such good men and treated the players so well.

Lucas wished he knew what his dad had said to Coach Earl when he explained the situation with Jessica being on the team. He assumed it went well since he didn't talk about it at home, and now he was curious how practice would go.

Coach Earl took the infielders with him and told those who wanted to play outfield to go with Coach Howard for fly balls. Coach Earl put the infielders in one line and hit them ground balls in turn. Each player scooped up the ball, threw it to the catcher beside Coach Earl, then trotted back to the end of the line. It was a drill Lucas remembered doing every year he had played. He didn't hold back his throws this time. A little extra hop followed by a grunt helped whip the ball sharply into the catcher's mitt. He thought he noticed Coach Earl pause like he was thinking after witnessing one of his throws.

Coach Earl said he wanted to try a round of infield where they put players in each position and hit balls they would field and throw to the bases like they would in a game. He told Timmy to go to first base, which was an obvious choice, and Jeff was told to play third. Bobby was already at catcher. Coach Earl then pointed his bat toward Jessica and told her to go to second base. Lucas's heart was in his throat, and he felt his chest squeeze a little. Coach Earl then placed the bat on his shoulder and turned toward Lucas.

"I've noticed you have a pretty strong arm, Lucas. You made some dandy throws during the tryouts, and I think you may have been throwing harder today. I don't know what your secret is, but maybe I could get you to share it with the team." He smiled and scanned the infield for a moment. "So, why don't you head on out there to shortstop and we'll get this round of infield started."

Coach Earl had sent him out so nonchalantly Lucas thought he might have been joking for a minute. Shortstop was the most important position in the infield, and Coach Earl acted like it was obvious Lucas would play there. He never imagined himself moving to shortstop. He wanted to be the top player picked but assumed someone else would be the shortstop while he played second base. He knew second base better than any other position.

He sprinted to the shortstop position and immediately began raking through the dirt with his cleats to smooth out the lumps like he saw the big-league shortstops do. He spat in the palm of his glove and rubbed it in with his fingers. He then pounded his fist into his glove a couple of times ready for the ground balls to be hit his way. Jeff had already thrown one over when Coach Earl cracked the next one to Lucas's left. He slid over, snagged the ball cleanly in his glove, then fired a sharp throw chest high to Timmy at first.

The rest of the practice was a dream. Ground balls, pop-ups, line drives, were all falling into Lucas's glove followed by a bullet to the appropriate base. Lucas's enthusiasm was rubbing off on the rest of the team, too. Players were shouting all the baseball lingo they knew to one another, and the practice was as crisp as any Lucas had ever seen. He never thought twice about Jessica being a girl on his baseball team.

Lucas got in the car with his dad after practice. "How'd it go?" his dad asked.

"Well, he wants me to play shortstop. I've always played second base."

"Shortstop is a promotion. He must see big things in you."

"You're probably right. That was the best practice I've ever been in. I think I'm going to like playing short after all."

The euphoric feeling lasted all the way until the bus ride to school the next day. Boys from the other teams immediately engulfed Lucas in his seat. Russ Ledbetter took a quick look toward the front of the bus before he leaned in to Lucas. "I heard Jessica took your position at second base. How's it feel getting beat out by a girl?"

"For your information, Bedwetter, I'm playing shortstop." He scrunched up his face to restrain some of his anger.

"Well, after Jessica took your spot, they had to put you somewhere."

This type of ribbing continued all the way to school. Each stop brought a new boy to the back of the bus where Ledbetter could repeat some of his previous insults. The bus pulled in front of the school and Lucas jumped up and started pushing his way forward. The driver made him sit back down while the younger kids exited first. A car pulled up behind the bus and stopped.

"Look, Lucas. There's the girl who took you out of your position. Watch out, she's going to come on the bus and take your seat!" said Ledbetter as the boys burst out in laughter.

Lucas darted off the bus and got lost in the crowd of kids entering the school. He arrived at his first period class and purposely chose a seat away from Jessica so he wouldn't give Ledbetter any more ammunition.

The social studies teacher, Ms. Kipp, was all excited as they were beginning their unit on the western states along the Pacific Ocean. She explained they were going to do an assignment with a partner requiring a written report and a visual aid about a different state in the region. A buzz began as students started signaling around the room for partners. "But the good news is…I'll be assigning your partners." Most teachers would have been met with a chorus of boos, but it somehow made sense when she explained it—didn't hurt that she was the youngest and prettiest teacher in school. "I've put everyone's name in this fishbowl, and I'll pull out two names of people who will work together and which state you get."

She started pulling out pairs of names, and the class reactions went from laughter to groans of jealousy.

Ms. Kipp reached into her fishbowl and grabbed a piece of paper. She opened it, smiled and closed it. She then reached in for a second one and repeated the same move. She had the entire class staring at her as she continued this dramatic pause. A couple of girls sat up higher in their desks and grabbed the tops. Ms. Kipp opened her eyes wide and slowly began to speak.

"Let's see. I have Lucas Billman," she said as she opened one paper, "and Jessica Snider," she said as she opened the other. "You guys will be working on Hawaii. Sounds like fun."

The boys around Lucas bit their lips, squeezing their mouths tight and looking at each other. He braced himself for whichever one would be the first one to blurt something out in his direction. Nobody spoke. Ms. Kipp walked behind the boys and slowed down to a stop right behind Russ. The boys all straightened in their seats.

Ms. Kipp explained the rest of the class period would be spent getting together with partners and organizing how to get the assignment completed. Lucas waved to Jessica to join him in the corner closest to Ms. Kipps desk. He turned his desk so he couldn't see the rest of the students in the room, then helped Jessica pull hers close.

"You are not going to believe this, Lucas, but we are already half done. Last year, at my old school, I had to do a science project on something from Hawaii, and I think it will work for this. I'm pretty sure we brought it with us when we moved." She reached up and tightened her ponytail making Lucas think she was ready to get to work.

"Great," replied Lucas quietly. "We've got this set of encyclopedias at my house. We could find enough about Hawaii in there for a good report."

"How about I bring the volcano from my project over to your house tonight? I'll show you how it works, we'll look up stuff in your encyclopedias, and be done with this thing right away. I can come over as soon as I get home from school."

"This sounds like it may be the easiest project I've ever had to do for school," replied Lucas. He turned in his seat to stare at the other pairs of students awkwardly trying to talk to each other to plan their projects. He leaned back over toward Jessica. "Look at some of these guys. You can tell by watching them now, they'll never figure out how to finish this. I'm looking forward to watching them squirm while we coast through."

⚾

"Hey, Lucas! Are both of you guys going to wear coconut bras for the presentation or just you?" asked Les, who was seated on the bus across the aisle from Russ, who was trying to hide behind the bus seat.

"Make sure you wear your grass skirt over your jeans. Nobody wants to see your underwear when you do the hula!" yelled Russ from his hidden spot. And Lucas thought the morning bus ride took a long time.

A few minutes after he came home, Jessica showed up in the driveway carrying a large box. Lucas let her into the house and to the basement where the encyclopedias rested on a shelf. He took the box from Jessica and set it on the ping-pong table. She took the lid off the box, revealing a homemade volcano resting in the middle of green moss. She also reached into the box and pulled out a small bottle of vinegar, orange food coloring, and an eyedropper.

"Watch this," announced Jessica. "You put in a couple of drops of the food coloring in the top and then add some vinegar." She reached down and drew a dropper full of the vinegar, then squirted it all in the top of the volcano. Immediately, an orange foamy substance appeared out of the top. It grew and began to ooze down the sides of the volcano and into the green moss.

"Whoa!" was all Lucas could muster. He kept watching foam continue to bubble out. "How did you do that?"

"There was already baking soda in the volcano. It reacts with the vinegar and makes the foam. The orange food coloring is to make it appear to be lava. It was my mom's idea. Luckily, she was making cupcakes for a party and had food coloring on the counter when we built this."

Lucas stared a little more until the foam stopped. He pulled out the V and H encyclopedias and put them on the table. In no time, they had put their heads together and churned out a report on "Volcanoes in Hawaii" with ease. They had completed this week-long assignment on the first day, and it wasn't even dark yet. Lucas had never worked so well with anyone else. Jessica was so cooperative with helping and not being demanding, Lucas had lost all memory of the needling he had taken earlier in the day.

His mom brought down some lemonade and her famous chocolate chip cookies. She set the plate down on the coffee table then asked Lucas, "I suppose you've already shown her the ball, haven't you?"

Lucas had nearly missed another tour. There had not been anyone new in the house since New Year's Eve. He reached up to the shelf and grabbed a slightly dirty baseball off the stand.

"My dad caught this ball hit by Roberto Clemente last year. Well, before Clemente died, that is." It was the first time Lucas had shown the ball since Clemente's death. He felt an awkward sense he hadn't felt before when telling the story. He handed the ball to Jessica. He didn't know what he was going to say if she asked why it was so dirty. Luckily, she didn't ask.

"We have a Clemente Ball, too," Jessica said with enthusiasm.

"Seriously? You guys caught a ball hit by Clemente?"

"No, he didn't hit it."

Lucas stared at Jessica a moment and was about to ask how they got the ball when Jessica finished her thought.

"He signed it. My dad bought it at some black-tie charity auction last year before Christmas. It said, *Feliz Navidad, Roberto Clemente.* Isn't it funny to say Merry Christmas in Spanish on a baseball? I've never touched it, though. My dad keeps it in a glass case in his study, and he would kill me or anyone else if he ever caught us with it. Something about it being invaluable now because it could be the last thing he ever signed. I don't know."

Lucas reached up, took the ball from Jessica, and returned it to the stand. His dirty baseball and funny story didn't seem as interesting now as a ball Clemente held in his hands and signed. He thought Jessica might find his ball on a homemade stand silly compared to a ball purchased from an auction and kept under glass. His mind was going blank trying to think of something to say to change the subject.

"I bet we have a good team this year," Jessica gave Lucas the break he couldn't create himself.

"Um, yeah. How'd you like practice last night?" asked Lucas.

"It was great! Do baseball practices always go like that?"

"My team last year stunk, so we never practiced like that," Lucas answered.

"I'd like to throw a little more before we practice tomorrow, but my dad won't be home until late." Jessica snapped her head up. "Hey, do you want to pass some baseball now? It's still light outside."

Lucas didn't feel like he could say no, so he went and got his glove, a baseball and his dad's glove for Jessica to use. They headed out to the front yard and made a few warmup tosses, gradually increasing the distance between them. The more they threw, the more Lucas relaxed. Jessica was a friendly girl and a good ball player. He had high hopes of playing alongside her this season. He felt good enough he was comfortable letting her in on a little secret.

"My dad has been showing me how to throw a curveball."

"Really? Let's see it."

"That's just it. I can't do it yet. Let me show you what I mean."

Lucas gripped the ball as his dad had shown him. He snapped his wrist as he released the ball and felt it glide smoothly over and around his index finger. The ball was on a trajectory heading straight toward Jessica's shoulder. The spinning of the ball then began to defy the Laws of Physics and change course in a direct downward path. Jessica was barely able to track the new direction with her glove as the ball entered the webbing just before it would have hit her right thigh, slightly above the knee. Jessica slowly examined her glove caressing a baseball. A smile crept across her face, connecting the dimples on each cheek.

"That was amazing!" Jessica gazed at her glove and back to Lucas two or three times before she reached in and pulled out the ball.

Suddenly, a raucous assault of kissing noises came from behind Lucas. He caught a glimpse of four bicycles rounding the corner carrying young riders who cackled as they continued to make kissing noises speeding away. He could only make out the face of the last rider, Russ Ledbetter.

Brian Croasmun

CHAPTER NINE

Lucas fastened the top button of his Donovan Trucking jersey and checked to see it was securely tucked into his matching pants. He tried to smooth out any wrinkles as he stood up straight and stared at himself in the mirror. He pulled on his blue hat with the DT on the front, adjusted it up and down, then squeezed the bill from both sides forming an arch in the middle. He opened the door to his bedroom just enough to poke out his head. He heard movement in the kitchen and headed that direction.

"Are you going to wear your uniform to eat breakfast? I made French toast." His mom turned back to the stove and flipped another piece of bread with her spatula. "I don't want you to get syrup all over it."

"I'll be careful. I'll tuck this napkin in my collar, and it will cover the front," answered Lucas.

He gobbled up the plateful in front of him, wiped his mouth, and got up to put his dishes in the sink. "Thanks, Mom. That was really good. How soon until we leave for the parade?"

"I think your dad wants to leave in about ten minutes. That should give you guys plenty of time to find your team and get lined up. Your last Opening Day parade. Are you excited?" She smiled as she wiped her hands on a dish towel.

Lucas smiled and nodded his head. "I want to get to playing some baseball. I've been practicing for a couple of months now; I want to play a game."

"Then let's get going and get the day started." His dad walked into the room holding his car keys.

They all climbed into the station wagon and pulled out of the driveway.

"This sure is beautiful weather for a parade and a ballgame," said his mom as she looked out the car window, turned back toward Lucas, and smiled.

"Expect the first pitch ceremony to take a little longer this year. It's an election year, so the mayor will want to give a long speech, I'm sure," replied his dad.

"I wonder who will get to catch the first pitch this year?" Lucas asked. "Do you think they might pick me this year?"

"You never know, Lucas," said his dad as they pulled into the parking lot behind the city building. "The mayor is supposed to pick someone at random, but it always seems like he picks one of the coach's sons or someone on the league board."

Lucas didn't say anything more. He didn't want to ruin the surprise if it was going to be him.

Donovan Trucking gathered at the bottom of the steps to the city building while Russ Ledbetter and the Simpson's Paint Shop team assembled across the street near the library. The other teams were along the corner by the bank.

Lucas turned his attention to the youngest teams in the league and laughed how some of their uniforms were too big, and their caps fit loosely over their heads. He remembered being in awe of the boys on the older teams and thought they were superstars. He imagined some of the kids noticing him like that now.

Russ lurked around the side of a telephone booth and peered around in every direction. He saw Lucas look in his way, smacked a couple of his teammates on the shoulders, and they all puckered their lips and blew kisses toward Lucas. He turned his head and pretended not to see.

"Those jerks," mumbled Lucas as his jaws clenched.

"I can't stand those guys." Jeff made a fist and rolled his eyes.

"Who are you talking about?" asked Jessica. She looked around at all the teams.

"Shhh! Ledbetter and his buddies. They think they are so good because their dads agreed to coach together and made their team loaded. Russ, Ernie, and Les all on the same team," answered Jeff as he shook his head. The tryouts were intended to prevent this, but the league was always searching for volunteer coaches and didn't want to turn anyone down, even if they had found a loophole in the rules.

The police chief sounded the siren on his squad car, and each team followed him down Main Street in order from the youngest teams to the oldest. Donovan Trucking brought up the rear.

The players smiled and waved to the people on the sidewalks as they marched down the street. Jeff shoved Timmy when Timmy pointed out Julie standing by the shoe store with her parents. A couple of players recognized their parents or grandparents as they passed by and waved.

The Donovan Trucking team came to a sudden stop.

"Look! It's Ms. Kipp standing by the post office," shouted Lucas.

"She's wearing shorts and a t-shirt," said Jeff. His eyes grew big as he continued to stare.

"Is that her dog?" asked Jessica. She covered her mouth with her hands. "He's so cute."

Timmy's upper lip curled into a sneer. "Why is she all sweaty?"

Lucas didn't think he had ever seen a teacher outside of school before, much less running around in gym clothes.

"Good luck, Donovan Trucking! I hope you win your game," Ms. Kipp shouted to the team as she waved and took off jogging the other way with her golden retriever running stride for stride. Most of the boys stood and stared as she went around the corner toward the city building. Lucas stared longer than anyone. He never realized how graceful she really was.

The entire team took off in a short sprint to catch back up with the rest of the parade. They rounded the corner and headed on to Field 3 where all the other teams were lining up in the outfield. It was a collage of different colored hats and uniforms, all clean and shiny for the first day of the season.

"Lucas, Lucas!" yelled Chuckie. He was five-years-old, lived just down the street from Lucas, and since he was with the tee-ball teams, he knew it was Chuckie's first parade. His big shirt was tucked into his equally large pants, so Lucas wasn't even sure which team he played for. He gave Chuckie a little wave as they marched past.

"He lives on my street. Hey, he lives on my street! That big kid, Lucas," Chuckie continued to say to everyone standing around him. Lucas's smile spread across his face. He had never been idolized at the parade before.

Bill Quinn stood on the pitcher's mound and talked into a squealing microphone with a short speech about team work and sportsmanship. At least those were the only words Lucas could understand since the players were in the outfield and the speakers were facing the crowd in the bleachers. He then handed the microphone to the mayor who continued speaking, but the players couldn't hear much at all. Lucas noticed a couple times the mayor stopped to laugh, yet most of the crowd did not.

The mayor talked much longer than Bill. Lucas had been warned by his dad that the mayor's speech would be long, since the mayor was running for re-election this year. His speech finally came to an end when Lucas noticed everyone in the crowd applauding and the mayor being handed a brand-new baseball. He then began rubbing his chin like he was thinking when he turned toward the teams in the older baseball league. Lucas started thinking it would be cool to be picked to run to home plate and catch the first pitch of the season in front of half the town. Since his dad was on the league board, Lucas thought the mayor was searching for him, so he wiggled between his teammates to be in front and clearly visible. The mayor's eyebrows raised, and a smile crept across his face as he turned to focus on the Donovan Trucking team. The mayor raised an arm, extended a long, bony finger forward and pointed toward the team.

"Jessica Snider, come and catch the first pitch of the 1973 season!"

"What?"

"You've got to be kidding me."

"They can't be serious."

Lucas couldn't tell who said what, even though he was sure it came from the other teams. Donovan Trucking players were the only ones to give any kind of positive response with some half-hearted clapping. Lucas watched many adults in the crowd turn to whisper to one another while many clapped without even watching the events unfolding on the field. Mr. and Mrs. Snider stood together by the light pole near the third base dugout and fidgeted with their Polaroid camera.

Lucas wanted to say something to his teammates, but he wasn't sure if they would understand. He hadn't realized how badly he wanted to catch the first pitch until his name wasn't called. He only had this season to have his name called to catch the ceremonial pitch, and it had been given to someone who'd never been in the parade before. He had let himself get excited because he thought his dad was hinting his name would be picked. His dad really didn't know who it would be. He wasn't mad at Jessica. She wasn't the one who had looked him over, but would he have been chosen if not for her?

Jessica made her way to the plate and squatted down in preparation. The mayor was demonstrative in his windup, then let fly a pitch that bounced two feet in front of the plate. Jessica made a good play to scoop up the ball and save the mayor the embarrassment of having his pitch roll all the way to the backstop. She brought the ball back to the mayor who turned her around, so they could pose for a picture. Mrs. Snider was able to get a picture right beside the guy from the county newspaper. The mayor put the ball into Jessica's glove, winked, and patted her on the shoulder. Mr. Snider approached the mayor with a firm handshake and a quick, "Thanks, Bob."

"So, Mr. Snider knows the mayor. No wonder," said Lucas low enough he was the only one to hear it. Lucas tried to put this moment behind him. He had to be ready for the first game that afternoon. This was going to be his season.

"Good game."
"Good game."
"Good game."
"Good game."
"Good game."

Lucas went through the post-game handshake line with a straight face covering a smile ready to burst. He had a double and a single, made every play in the field, and they won their first game 6-3. He had even been a little startled in his last at-bat when he heard the coach for Conner's Market yell to his outfielders, "Back up, good hitter here!" Nobody had ever backed up their outfielders before when Lucas came to bat. It turned out to be good strategy when they caught a fly ball Lucas hit to centerfield.

"Gommmph gammmph," said Jessica through a mouthful of ice from her complimentary sno-cone the concession stand offered. "I mean, good game," after she swallowed the mouthful of frozen purple.

"You, too. Nice hit," answered Lucas, reaching for a blue sno-cone. Even though she had struck out her first two times, Jessica knocked a single up the middle in her last turn at bat, bringing the team to their feet in the dugout in a spontaneous ovation. As Lucas stood clapping with his teammates, he thought again this might be quite a season.

"We'll see you next game and see how good you and your girlfriend really are," said Russ Ledbetter as he and the Simpson's Paint Shop team passed Lucas to take the field for their game.

"Maybe I'll just stay home since you already know you're going to win," answered Lucas.

Lucas and Donavan Trucking did show up the next week, and as Russ predicted, they found out how good they really were. The game was so out of hand, Lucas was asked to come in to pitch the last inning. His arm felt strong, but they were already behind 15-6, so Lucas found it hard to focus on getting the ball over the plate.

"Ball four, take your base," yelled the umpire as Les trotted to first.

A pop-up to Jessica at second for the first out.

"Ball four." Another walk.

"Ball four," said the umpire, who sounded disappointed when he spoke. The bases were loaded.

Ernie stepped to the plate as Lucas took a deep breath. He reared back and let the pitch fly. It skipped off the dirt in front of the batter's box and bounced off of Ernie's shin.

"Ow!" Ernie yelled as he grabbed his leg.

"Take your base."

The score was now, 16-6, as Russ took his turn, laughing as he stepped in to hit.

Lucas rubbed the ball in his bare hands as he imagined himself throwing to the steps on the front porch. He had to settle down and throw a strike. He pictured himself in the bottom of the ninth of game seven of the 1971 World Series. He was once again Steve Blass.

Crack.

Lucas turned quickly to see where the ball was headed. It sailed over the left field fence, across the walking path, over the small bank, and onto the road out of the park. A grand slam home run. Russ laughed as he ran the bases.

Simpson's Paint Shop won the game, 20-6.

"The great thing about baseball," explained Coach Earl after the game, "is no matter how bad you get beat, you still get to play your next game. We'll be back here Friday evening and find out."

Coach Earl had been right. Donovan Trucking won Friday, then the next two games that followed.

The rematch with Simpson's Paint Shop went about the same way the first game did. Russ with another monster home run and a big lead late in the game.

In the bottom of the fifth inning, Wesley was on first and took off for second when the ball bounced away from the catcher. The throw came quickly but wide of the base. Jessica stretched out to catch the throw and swiped her glove in desperation to make a play. Her glove hit Wesley squarely in the face.

"He's out," yelled the umpire.

"What are you doing? You don't smack someone in the face with the tag," shouted Wesley.

"Settle down, Wesley. It was the only play she had," said Lucas as he stepped in toward Wesley.

"You busted my lip!"

"Don't worry. You weren't going to be kissing anyone this weekend, anyway," replied Lucas.

Donovan Trucking trotted off the field toward their dugout. Jessica caught up to Lucas right before they stepped over the baseline and patted him on the back with her glove.

"Thanks, Lucas."

"Oh, sure. He needs to quit complaining. He knows you can't help that kind of stuff."

"I wish you would have smacked him a little harder," laughed Jeff.

Jessica smiled, spit into her glove, punched her fist into it, and rubbed it back and forth.

Lucas had a new confidence in his team.

The rest of the regular season followed the same pattern. Donovan Trucking won game after game, except when they faced Simpson's Paint Shop. It was still the most fun Lucas ever had playing baseball.

Now Lucas only had one goal in mind; keep Simpson's Paint Shop from winning the championship. He was confident Donovan Trucking was the second-best team in the league. It was his job to make them the best.

Brian Croasmun

CHAPTER TEN

"We've got A-1 Construction for our first playoff game on Monday evening," announced Coach Earl after the last game. "Playoffs are lots of fun. You never know what's going to happen because it doesn't matter what happened in the regular season. The only wins that count now are the ones in the playoffs. We want to win that big team trophy, so Lucas's dad has to find a place for it down at the office. Of course, you can win individual trophies, too."

Lucas was excited all weekend looking forward to Monday. School was out, he had his days to himself, and his evenings to play baseball. Monday's plan was to sleep in, rest up, and get ready for the playoff game, which he felt was their championship game since nobody was going to beat Simpson's Paint Shop. A second-place trophy would still look nice.

Boom. Boom-boom. Boom. Boom-boom-boom.

Lucas was awakened by the sound of thunder. He came out of his room and saw his mom peeking out of the living room curtain.

"I guess you heard the storm," said his mom.

"Yeah, it's pretty loud. You don't think it will cancel the game, do you?" Lucas asked.

"It's supposed to clear out this afternoon. Maybe it will dry up in time."

Lucas was downstairs watching gameshows an hour later when the phone rang.

"We were afraid of that. I'll tell him," he heard his mom say. "Lucas."

"Game canceled?" Lucas yelled up the steps.

"Yep. You'll play tomorrow."

Eventually, the skies cleared, and warm air filled the neighborhood. It was a shame to not be playing when the weather was so nice now. But he knew the infield would be a mess, and he didn't want to have a playoff game on a wet ballfield. He decided to wait on the porch until his dad got home from work to tell him the news.

"Got rained out, did ya'?" his dad asked. "Seems a shame with it being so nice out there now. We'll get 'em tomorrow, I suppose. What are you doing right now?"

"Waiting to tell you the game was rained out," laughed Lucas.

"Would you want to go out and pass some baseball? You know, get the old arm ready for the playoffs?" his father asked.

"Yeah, sure," answered Lucas, even though he was thinking about watching some TV in the basement.

Lucas went to the closet to grab his glove and his dad's old one while he changed out of his work clothes. His dad came out a minute later wearing a Donovan Trucking company hat and an old grey t-shirt.

Lucas was handing a glove to his dad when he held up a finger and said, "Wait here a second. I have an idea."

His dad disappeared down the basement steps and came back holding a slightly used baseball. They didn't keep any baseball equipment down there, so there was only one ball it could be.

"Is that the Clemente Ball? What are you going to do with it?"

His dad wiggled his eye brows. "I'm going to help you become a better baseball player with it, that's what."

But the ball was special. He didn't catch it himself, but he had become something of a local celebrity because of it. How was it going to make him be a better baseball player? Shouldn't they keep it clean and safe?

"I had an idea, Lucas. I've been thinking about a lot of things lately." His dad sat down in the chair across from the recliner. "Ever since I told you about how I felt after Clemente died, I started thinking this ball could be even more special than a little trophy on the shelf above the basement TV."

Lucas sat down in the recliner.

"I thought we would take the Clemente Ball, as you like to call it, outside and throw it around. Think about this; it is a major-league quality baseball only hit one time, right?"

"Yea, they put it in the game right before you caught it."

"Exactly. Plus, this isn't the kind of thing we would ever sell. Nobody is going to be searching for a foul ball they want to add to their collection. It might be different if Clemente had autographed it or something, but he didn't. So, this ball is going to mean the most to you and me. Everyone else won't care much once they've heard the story of how we got it. Have any of your friends asked to see it twice?"

Lucas thought for a moment and shook his head.

"This can be a thing for only you and me to share. We'll take the ball hit by my favorite player, and I'm sure would have been your Grandpa's favorite player, and we'll use it when you and I pass baseball."

"Clemente was my favorite player, too." Lucas felt like he had to interject into this part of the discussion.

"Then it's settled. This one baseball is going to be the connection between me, you, our favorite player, and the grandfather you never knew. We can think about both of them as we get your arm in shape for the playoffs."

"Do you think Grandpa got to meet Clemente yet in Heaven?"

They stared at each other for a moment, then the corner of his dad's mouth began to curl up slowly. He turned back toward Lucas as his eyes became moist and glassy.

"I'm going to guess Grandpa has found him by now."

"I bet Grandpa told him all about you catching the ball. Maybe it was Grandpa who helped you catch it. Nobody believed you caught it by yourself."

His dad took in a deep breath and let it slowly out his nose.

"I think you may be right, Lucas. I think you may be right."

They went through their regular warmup routine, even though they had not been out to throw together much during the regular season. After numerous tosses, Lucas had made his way to the long throws and was about ready to call it quits.

"Want to try the curveball one more time?" his dad asked. He tapped his glove once, then held it open toward Lucas.

"No, I doubt I pitch in the playoffs, and I haven't been able to get it anyhow." Lucas shook his head and giggled. "Maybe after the season when I want to start practicing for when I move up to the older league next year."

"If you say so. The one thing you have to always plan for in the playoffs is that something unplanned will happen," his dad replied.

Lucas liked for his dad to think he understood his advice, but... "What do you mean?"

"I mean, no matter what you plan and practice to happen, there is going to be something to surprise you when the game is on the line. A bad player will make a great play, or a great player will make a bad play. It might happen to both teams; it might happen to one. That's what makes it so fun. Remember Hank down at the office? The only home run he ever hit in his life won the conference championship when were in high school."

"That skinny guy?" Lucas reached up and adjusted his cap.

"Yep. He says he still doesn't know how it happened. I remember it like it was yesterday." He stroked his moustache and stared in the distance a moment.

Lucas started daydreaming about what unexpected thing might happen in the playoffs. He was a good player. Maybe he would be the good player who makes a good play, instead.

Early Tuesday evening, most of the team had arrived in the dugout. Bobby grabbed a bat and practiced his swing. Jeff, Timmy and Danny played a game where they tried to keep a ball in the air by hitting it with the outside of their gloves. Nobody was sitting quietly in the dugout.

Coach Earl called Lucas over to him by the bat rack. "Lucas, we've been figuring out how we can win this whole tournament, and we've decided we need you to pitch a couple innings today to save some of the innings Timmy and Jeff can throw, since the league has a weekly innings limit. If you give us two good innings at the start, we should be able to get through the rest with the other two. Think you can do it?"

"I'll try my best," Lucas answered.

Coach Earl handed him a new baseball. "Here's the game ball for tonight. Head over and warm up with Bobby."

Coach Earl walked away, and Lucas let out a heavy sigh. Of all the things he imagined doing in the playoffs, being the starting pitcher, even if only for a couple innings, was the last thing he thought he would do.

His first warmup throw skipped across the ground in front of Bobby, and the second one almost sailed over his head. He hoped his two innings would go quickly and Donovan Trucking would be in the lead when they took him out.

Coach Earl called the team together.

"Lucas will pitch the first couple innings so Jeff and Timmy can pitch today and in the championship game, when we'll need them the most," he explained.

"What if he has a no-hitter going? Are you still going to take him out?" Jessica asked. Everyone, including Lucas and the coaches laughed. Jessica had overheard the earlier conversation with Coach Earl.

"We'll worry when the time comes, Jessica," Coach Earl answered.

Jeff slid over to shortstop while Lucas went to the pitcher's mound after throwing his warmup pitches. Two ground balls and an easy pop-up later had Lucas heading for the dugout after a three-up-three-down inning. Jessica trotted by Lucas on their way to the dugout. "You've got a no-hitter going." She chuckled.

I guess I do have a no-hitter going.

Lucas knocked Jeff in with a single, then Timmy hit a double to chase home. Lucas and Donovan Trucking was ahead 2-0 after the first inning.

Lucas went to the mound hoping they would still be ahead after he finished his last inning. The first three batters all hit weak ground balls for three easy outs. Jessica fielded two of the balls. She waited until they reached the dugout before making her announcement this time, "Lucas still has a no-hitter going. Are you taking him out, Coach?"

A slow grin stretched across Coach Earl's face as he headed out to third base. A couple more runs came in and it was 4-0 after the second inning.

Lucas was now a little confused. He had done his job, but he was feeling strong as a pitcher tonight. He jogged out of the dugout but made sure to slow down when he got near the mound. Coach Earl didn't say a word as he was coming the other way. He merely stretched out his hand toward the pitching rubber and nodded his head toward Lucas.

An extra shot of adrenaline was now racing through his body. Lucas confidently stepped to the mound as he knew the bottom of the batting order was due. He struck out two of the batters and fielded a slow little grounder to retire the other batter himself. He didn't even need the rest of the team that inning. His confidence was soaring. Of course, Jessica boosted it more. "It's still a no-hitter."

For the first time this game, Lucas sat down in the dugout. He wasn't up to bat for a while. A thought came racing to his head from a few weeks ago when his father showed him another baseball article in the newspaper. Nolan Ryan had thrown his first ever no-hitter in the major leagues. "It's unbelievable how hard that guy throws, they say. And his curveball…" said his dad as he shook his head.

"Why does he look so lonely on the bench? I'd think he would be happy," asked Lucas, staring at the picture of a solitary player in the dugout.

"It's an old baseball superstition. You don't talk to the pitcher about his no-hitter, so you don't jinx him. It's crazy what those big leaguers will do. He's probably thinking about all the pressure of throwing a no-hitter."

Lucas noticed he was the only one sitting on the bench now. Not because his team believed they would jinx him, but because Timmy just hit the longest home run they had ever seen hit on their field. Lucas snapped out of his thoughts in time to congratulate Timmy as he walked into the dugout.

"What did it feel like when you hit it, Timmy?" asked Jessica.

"I don't know. I didn't feel anything at all. I just swung hard and the ball went flying," Timmy answered.

Sweet spot. Another one of his dad's favorite baseball terms.

For two more innings Lucas went to the mound, and for two more innings, A-1 Construction didn't get a hit. Everyone knew this because Jessica never failed to announce it when they went into the dugout. So much for a jinx.

Donovan Trucking had built up an 8-0 lead by the end of the fifth inning, and Lucas was having the most fun he'd ever had playing baseball. One more inning, three more outs, and he would have a no-hitter. And they would be in the championship game.

The first batter proved to be a little feisty. He fouled off pitch after pitch. Lucas tried throwing harder and harder but couldn't get one by him. Finally, on the eighth pitch, he popped up a ball Lucas snatched out of the air with ease.

Lucas took a big sigh of relief after that struggle. He stepped up to the pitching rubber a little more relaxed. He went through his wind up, let the ball fly and CRACK! The ball came off the hitter's bat heading right toward Jessica. The ball continued to climb. Jessica leapt, her glove high in the air, before falling to the ground. She looked down into her opened glove. There was nothing there. The ball dropped into the outfield grass and rolled to the right fielder. A-1 Construction had their first base hit.

Lucas bent over and put his hands on his knees as he saw Jessica punch her glove. She acted more disappointed than he was. Jeff took the throw from the outfield and flipped the ball to Lucas.

"Come on, we've got to get these last two outs so we can be in the championship," said Jeff.

With the pressure off, Lucas fired the first two pitches right past the next batter. As he took the throw back from the catcher, a thought hit him. *Let's give the curveball a try.* "What is there to lose now?" he said out loud to himself.

He lined up his middle finger on the threads, wound up, snapped his wrist, and let the ball fly. It was heading right for the plate, shoulder high to the batter. It then darted straight down, and the batter swung and missed it by a foot. The umpire even let out a weak, "Strike three," as he was still processing what he saw.

The last batter wrapped the game up quickly. He swung at the first pitch and hit an easy pop-up to Jessica at second base. She squeezed the ball in her glove and Donovan Trucking was heading to the championship game. The team ran off the field and Jessica pulled up next to Lucas.

"Here's another ball for your basement shelf. Try not to get them mixed up," Jessica said as she stuck the ball into Lucas's glove.

The teams met at home plate for the traditional handshakes, then Coach Earl gathered the team together. "Where did the game ball get to?"

Lucas opened his glove to reveal the ball.

"You keep it," Coach Earl said. "That's why I wanted it. Great job, Lucas, great job. Listen, guys. We play in the championship game next week and Jeff and Timmy still have all their innings to pitch. I think this gives us a great chance. We are going to have a practice on Thursday morning at nine o'clock so you can have the rest of the day for yourselves."

"We'll make sure they're here, Coach," said a parent from the back of the group.

A few parents giggled. Lucas was puzzled. He wasn't sure, but it looked like Coach Earl winked to the group.

"What's so funny about having practice?" Lucas whispered to Jessica.

"I have no idea," she answered.

Lucas shrugged his shoulders and took a moment to open his glove to look at the ball again. He reached in with his right hand, spun it around, pulled it out, and flicked it back in the glove before closing it shut. He remembered what his dad had said about something unexpected happening in the playoffs. A bad pitcher just had a great game. Now, he wondered what was in store for the championship game.

CHAPTER ELEVEN

Lucas was stretched out on the basement couch watching game shows and enjoying the relaxing pace of the summer break from school while occasionally glancing up at the ball resting on the shelf above the TV, his second one on the mantle in the living room upstairs. Eventually, Lucas planned to display them together in the basement. Even though the championship game was next week, he was taking a little break from baseball this morning. His arm felt like one of those butcher shop sausages hanging from up high, swaying with the wind. In all the excitement of the playoff victory, he hadn't noticed it was the most he had ever pitched at one time. He had already decided to tell his dad no if he suggested they pass baseball today.

"Lucas, I think Jessica is riding her bike up the driveway. Were you expecting her to come over?" yelled his mom down the basement stairs.

"What does she want?" yelled Lucas up the stairs as he sat up on the couch.

"How do I know? I'm sure she didn't ride her bike all the way over here to visit me. Why don't you get up here and find out?" his mom replied as the doorbell began to ring.

Lucas sprinted up the steps and opened the door.

Jessica started talking before he could even get out a greeting. "I'm guessing you didn't stay around for the other playoff game last night, did you? Of course not, or you would be riding over to my house to tell me the news. Get out here."

"My parents took me to Dairy Queen to celebrate after the game. My dad said he needed a milkshake to calm his stomach after the game because a sno-cone couldn't cut it." Lucas laughed as Jessica rolled her eyes playfully. They both sat down on the front porch chairs.

"Get this. While our game was going on last night, Simpson's Paint Shop was out hanging around the swings at the park after they warmed up. Ledbetter was fooling around standing on a swing, then fell off and broke his arm. I guess he was laying out there screaming and crying while Timmy hit his home run, so we didn't notice it."

Lucas's eyes grew large as he dropped his head in disbelief.

"That's not everything. His parents had to run him to the hospital, so Ernie's dad had to be head coach."

"You mean big mouth, Curtis? I heard my dad once say he has such a big mouth because he always has to talk over the chainsaw he uses trimming trees." Lucas laughed but Jessica was scooting to the edge of her seat.

"That's still not all the news. Ernie had to pitch since Russ was out, and he couldn't throw the ball over the plate. His dad kept yelling at him and yelling at the umpire. Pretty soon they were behind like ten runs because he wouldn't take Ernie out. They got beat!

Conner's Market killed them." Lucas furrowed his brow as he tried to process all this information.

"Are you listening to me? Simpson's Paint shop lost! They are out of the playoffs. We only need to beat Conner's Market for the championship, and we beat them every time this year."

A grin started to spread across Lucas's face. Then, a laugh bubbled up in his belly, worked its way up his chest, and out of his mouth. He let out a couple more chuckles as he leaned back in his chair. "Unbelievable."

Mike appeared walking across the yard and joined them on the front porch.

"You're not going to believe what happened to Ledbetter last night," Lucas said.

"As long as it's something bad," replied Mike as he smirked.

Lucas repeated Jessica's story and they all had another laugh at Ledbetter's misfortune.

"Hey, how'd you guys do?" asked Mike.

Lucas paused a moment before he took in a breath to start telling the game story. Jessica cut him off and began to describe the game with much more vigor than Lucas could show. He leaned back in the chair and listened as she described each play and watched as Mike smiled and turned his head occasionally toward Lucas with a nod and a raise of his eyebrows. Lucas tried to hide his smile, but the corners of his mouth insisted on pushing up his face.

"Count on me coming to this championship game next week," said Mike.

Lucas remained on the porch for a few minutes after Mike and Jessica had left when his dad pulled up the driveway from work. Lucas was starting to stand up as his dad reached the top step. "I've already heard, son, if that's what you're waiting for. Just between us, the guys in the league are kind of happy about it. They never did like the way those dads twisted the rules to load up a team, when that is exactly why we go to all the trouble to do the tryouts in the first place."

"We kind of feel the same way," Lucas answered.

"How's the chicken wing feel today? I bet it's pretty tired. It's probably the most pitches you've ever thrown. I don't think you could have gone much further."

"I'm glad we don't play today. I don't think I could make the throw from shortstop."

"That's normal. It'll start coming around tomorrow. You should be fine to play in the championship game. That's why the starters in the big leagues only pitch about once a week. Your arm needs the rest today. I was afraid you were going to want to throw the Clemente Ball around when I got home," his dad said with a wink.

"I didn't even go swimming today. I didn't think it would work with one arm."

"You'd have swum around in circles." They both chuckled. "We can pass the Clemente Ball around later. It's not like we're going to go anywhere when you've got the big championship game coming up next week. I'm really looking forward to seeing it."

"And I can't wait to play in it."

116

CHAPTER TWELVE

The players began arriving to the parking lot at the field a little before nine o'clock. Some were barely awake and had obviously thrown on a hat and hopped in the car. However, Lucas noticed every single face had a smile or a grin, no matter how tired they may have felt. The trash cans around the field were overflowing, and there was still quite a bit of garbage around the bleachers and the fences. He thought there must have been some kind of a party here this week. He then smiled to himself.

The players were all standing in a small group shuffling gravel with their feet while a couple of the parents had stayed around as the team waited.

"Hey, where are the coaches?" asked Jeff.

"What's the point in having an early practice if we are going to start late?" asked Jessica.

Both of their questions were answered at once. The biggest white van any of the players had ever seen pulled into the parking lot with Coach Earl behind the wheel and Coach Howard riding shotgun. Coach Earl gave the horn a couple of honks as Coach Howard hopped out and pulled open the big side door.

The parents that were still around began laughing and clapping. The players looked at each other, then they began smiling and laughing. Lucas joined in having no idea why.

"We have a big surprise for you kids and your parents are all in on it," Coach Earl announced to the group. "We aren't having practice today. We wanted to this after the championship game, but I have to leave town on business the next day, so we thought we'd do this early."

The players continued to look around at the smiling adults. Danny's mom held her hand over her mouth trying to cover her laughing smile.

"What is it? Why are you guys all so happy? Why aren't we having practice?" Jessica asked.

"Coach Howard and I are taking you kids to Kennywood Park!" yelled Coach Earl.

"Yeah!"

"Woohoo!"

"Cool!"

"This is why we brought the van. This is a treat form me and Coach Howard. We just wanted to thank you kids for giving us a great season. It's going to be just us and you players."

"No parents?" Timmy asked.

"Nope, just the coaches," answered Coach Howard.

"Yeah!" cheered the team in unison. The parents chuckled in the parking lot.

"Pile in and we'll get headed to the park," said Coach Earl.

"Are we all going to fit in here?" Lucas poked his head in the van and scanned the seats.

"I think you'll see there is plenty of room," answered Coach Howard.

Jessica hopped in first and went to the back row, followed by Lucas, Jeff, and Bobby. The other players filled in and found they had plenty of room for everyone. Coach Howard slid the door closed and announced to the parents, "We'll drop everyone off at their house before it gets too late."

"Next stop, Kennywood Park!" yelled Coach Earl as he turned back from the front seats. A cheer went up from the team. "It's time to celebrate a great season!" An even bigger cheer followed.

Jessica was seated by one window with Bobby by the other. Lucas and Jeff squeezed easily into the middle of the spacious back seat. Jessica was staring out of the window toward the field as they pulled out, and Lucas wondered if she was still thinking about Tuesday night like he was. Lucas had stared at his ceiling trying to fall asleep for a long while after getting home from the game and replayed most of the highlights of the night through his head. He awoke this morning from the deepest sleep he'd had in a while and finally came out to gaze at the game ball sitting on the fireplace mantle. He hadn't been dreaming.

He was trying to drum up the courage to ask Jessica if that's what she was doing now when she broke the silence.

"Which rollercoaster do you want to ride first? I've never been to Kennywood before. What's the best thing to ride?"

"Thunderbolt. You have to ride the Thunderbolt. It's the biggest coaster I've ever ridden."

It was a pretty easy admission for Lucas. Kennywood was the only amusement park he had ever visited. His family had come once before, and his parents didn't enjoy the coasters much. His sisters had run off together to find some friends, leaving Lucas to ride with strangers most of the day. It was not fun. He hoped having all of his teammates around would give him the courage to enjoy the day and face the rollercoasters he feared.

Coach Howard stood watching all the players squirm in the parking lot while they waited for Coach Earl to get back with their tickets. Nobody could stand still or keep their hands to themselves. They poked, prodded, shoved, and elbowed each other with a belly laugh in between. The group finally settled down when Coach Earl came walking back with a fistful of tickets.

"Listen up everyone, we've got some ground rules for you guys to follow today so you can have plenty of fun and we don't lose anyone. Now Coach Howard and I don't fit into these rides quite like we used to." Coach Howard patted his belly and let out a laugh. "You may not see us on too many of these roller coasters. We know you guys won't all want to ride the same rides all day, so we've decided to follow the buddy system. Everyone must have a buddy from the team with them all day long. It doesn't have to be the same one all the time, but don't leave the group unless someone is going with you. This way it will be easier to round you guys up quickly."

"I'll be your buddy, Lucas," said Jessica. He hadn't even had a second to think he needed to recruit himself a buddy yet, and now he was being asked to commit by the only girl in the whole traveling party.

"Sure, yea, I guess." Lucas scanned through the team and decided he would have chosen Jessica, anyway. They always got along well, and he hoped she would be a little shy about riding some of the big rides like he knew he would be.

The rest of the team paired up into "buddies" and prepared to start out on their day of adventure. Coach Earl pulled everyone in close one last time before turning them loose.

"Everyone back here to this spot at 12:30 for lunch. Then you will have the rest of the day to catch anything you might have missed this morning. Now go have some fun!"

"Let's go to the Thunderbolt!" yelled Jeff. The mob took off in a sprint toward the most feared rollercoaster in the park. They pushed, shoved, and laughed all the way to the line forming outside of the ride. Bobby beat everyone there, but Lucas was toward the front of the group. He looked over his left shoulder searching for Jessica, not realizing she was on his right side finishing the run over in almost the same time. He had hoped to have built up some courage by this time, but his nervousness had only increased.

The line moved quickly, since the park was still filling up with customers for the day. The team had made it to the front of the line as the next coaster came to a screeching halt. The pushing, shoving, and laughing continued as they all jumped on board. Lucas climbed across to the seat on the right side and started to sit down when he noticed Jessica had squeezed through a couple boys to get the seat to his left.

"Here we go, buddy. You scared?" asked Jessica.

Yes, terrified.

"Not at all. I've ridden this before," answered Lucas as he began to squeeze the safety bar as hard as he could. He closed his eyes and took a deep breath before the wheels started to turn.

The coaster began to move and immediately started its slow climb up the first hill. Lucas stared forward and was a little relieved when he heard Jessica let out a scream. He peeked over enough to find Jessica with her hands in the air letting out another scream.

"Woooooohoooooo! Let's go!" she yelled straight up into the sky as the coaster reached its apex. It paused for a moment at the top before taking off like a flash straight down. Lucas could no longer hear anything but the sound of the wind whooshing past his ears as the coaster began to twist and turn rapidly. Up and down, side to side, went the direction of the tracks. His body was pinned to the back of his seat. His grip tightened and he tried to open his eyes once again to catch a peek of Jessica. His eyes closed quickly when Jessica's flailing right arm came across his forehead as the coaster made a sharp turn to the left before screeching down the last straight stretch to end the ride. The safety bar released, and Lucas finally felt safe enough to completely open his eyes to take in his surroundings.

Jessica hopped out of her seat and paced back and forth waiting for Lucas to get up. He was already rethinking his choice of buddy.

The team exited to the side and came to a fast consensus.

"Let's ride it again!" shouted Bobby.

Lucas was not ready to ride again. He tried to come up with an excuse to get out of going on the Thunderbolt a second time this soon. His mind kept drawing a blank. The group had started to head toward the ride when inspiration struck.

"I have to go to the bathroom. You guys go ahead, I'll catch the next one," Lucas said.

"Nope, buddy," replied Jessica. "I can't let you do that."

"I'll just be a minute. Go ahead, I'll catch up."

"Nope. I don't want to keep riding the same thing. Let's head over that way and you can go into the restroom over there. I'll wait outside."

Lucas went inside the restroom and stopped at the sink. He stared into the mirror and looked at himself. This was the kid who was suddenly thrown into pitching a playoff game, then threw a one-hitter and he was afraid of rollercoasters. The only thing he feared more than rollercoasters was all of his teammates finding out he was afraid of rollercoasters.

He splashed a little water on his face and went out the door to tell Jessica he didn't want to ride anymore rollercoasters.

"Look, the log ride is right over here. Let's go ride that next," Jessica interrupted his thought before he could say anything.

"Where is it?" Lucas asked. He tried to stall in order to think of a way out of it.

"Right there, see?" she said as she pointed ahead. "I thought you'd been here before."

"Oh, yeah. I forgot."

Jessica started to walk toward the log ride. Lucas had to either speak up or follow along. He followed.

The line was short, so they hopped in the next log rolling up. Lucas was much more relaxed when boarding this ride and could lean back comfortably in his seat when the safety bar came down and they started to pull away. Jessica didn't feel the need to wave her hands in the air at the start of this one, either. Lucas noticed a slight clench in his stomach once the log engaged with the chain pulling it up the first hill, but he was able to keep sitting back so Jessica didn't notice. The shorter trip to the top helped ease the tightness.

"Woohoo!" Jessica's hands went back up in the air. Lucas started to clench the safety bar.

They went flying down the first hill with a big splash at the bottom. The water went sideways and didn't get them wet, which Jessica answered with an, "Awwww."

Another quick hill and an even smaller splash came right before a couple of twists and turns to each side, before they went under the waterfall. Jessica crossed her arms over her face, not realizing the water was shot across the tracks so the riders thought they were going to get drenched but didn't.

Lucas could feel the clicking of the log connecting with the chain below, which meant the ride was heading up the final big hill where the last splash was sure to soak everyone. He put his hands tighter around the safety bar across his lap. Jessica had since dropped her arms from the near miss at the waterfall. Lucas glanced toward her and she was leaning back without a care. Lucas leaned to his left and quietly told her, "You better hang on because…here…we…GO!"

The last word had flown out of Lucas's mouth as the log went screaming down the hill. Water shot up both sides. A couple of quick turns and all the passengers had water falling on their heads. Up and down another short hill brought back the speed they were losing when the log came shooting down the last stretch, causing a wall of water to cascade over the group, leaving everyone soaked. Lucas let go of the safety bar before Jessica could wipe the water from her face and turn toward him, water dripping from her nose and chin.

"That was incredible! I wasn't ready for the last rush until you warned me," Jessica said.

"I didn't think you were. See why I told you?" answered Lucas. He knew, in truth, he was telling himself. He wasn't even sure he had said the warning out loud.

"What's next?" Jessica asked.

Lucas summoned the courage to ride the old wooden rollercoaster called the Jack Rabbit before heading to meet the team for lunch. He used this time to not only fill his stomach, but to think of a way to not ride anymore rollercoasters.

"Let's go play some midway games," suggested Lucas to the team.

Some of the team agreed with Lucas and went to the midway, while the rest left in search of more rides.

"Here we go, throwing baseballs at milk jugs. We ought to be able to win something here, Mr. No-hitter?" she asked.

"Mr. One-hitter, if you don't mind."

The rules were simple. Three balls for a chance to knock down three jugs. Each jug downed won a bigger prize. The problem was the jugs must have been full of cement since they were so heavy and didn't move easily. Some other patrons ahead of them had hit the jugs near the neck and the ball glanced off. Plus, they had to use the softest baseballs any of them had ever felt.

"I'm going for the purple bear up there, Lucas. I need to knock down two out of the three. I think I can do it," said Jessica.

The first throw sailed right over the top of everything. Lucas laughed and Jessica pursed her lips.

Her second throw hit below the neck of the left bottle. The bottle teetered back and finally fell flat on its back.

"That's more like it," said Jessica sternly.

Jessica started to clench her teeth and rub down the ball for her last throw. She took a deep breath before rearing back to make her final attempt. A grunt escaped her mouth as the ball exited her hand. It hit squarely on the neck of the right jug. The bottle wobbled a moment,

126

leaned back, and settled right back in an upright position. Jessica pounded her fist into her hand like she did when the only hit in the playoff game floated over her glove. Lucas watched as she reluctantly accepted the small stuffed monkey for her prize.

Lucas wiggled his arm for a moment to decide if it was over the soreness from pitching earlier this week. It seemed like such a long time ago, but some of the soreness was still there. He didn't want to be left out, but he also didn't want to miss and be embarrassed in front of everybody. He thought he had enough strength to give it a try.

His first throw went between the necks of the right and middle jugs. It made enough contact to make them move without showing any chance of falling over. He shook his head, then wiggled his arm as if to loosen it up a bit more. The second throw felt good coming out of his hand and hit the middle jug smack in the center. Immediately, it flew back and fell to the table with a thud.

"Wow, good throw," said the man in charge of the game as he whistled to the crowd. "Look here, folks! This guy just guaranteed a prize and now is going for the bigger ones on the top shelf. You can be next, right after his next throw."

Jessica had been to the side still shaking her head when Lucas missed the first throw but popped her head up when she heard the thud from the second. The rest of the group began to gather closer before the last one.

Lucas held the ball for a second and was momentarily lost in thought. He was picturing taking the mound in the first playoff game, watching the next-to-last batter swing and miss at his curveball, and visiting with his dad after the game over a milkshake.

A smile then crossed his face as he let fly with his final throw.

He aimed it at the right jug Jessica couldn't knock down on her throw. The ball hit flush, but at the top of the neck, much like Jessica's. However, the jug leaned back and fell with a thud as loud as the last one. A small cheer went up from the team, including a smile from Jessica.

"Those aren't supposed to fall when you hit there. I don't think I've ever seen that before. You must have put something into your throw. Which prize would you like? Anything from this side wall over here," said the man in charge of the game.

"How about the purple bear?"

The man reached up, pulled down a large purple bear, and handed it to Lucas who immediately turned and handed it to Jessica.

"Here, trade you. I like monkeys better," he said as he thrust the bear into her hands while taking the small monkey. He quickly turned and headed for some other games. Jessica was stunned for a moment as she received the purple bear. She stared at it, gave it a squeeze and started to follow Lucas, along with some others on the team.

It wasn't long until the team loaded the van for the ride home. A day in the sun had drained most of the energy they had that morning. The chatter was low, and a few of the players, including Jessica, had fallen asleep in their seats. Lucas leaned back and enjoyed the quiet after a stressful day.

A couple of players had already been dropped off at their homes when the van turned the corner heading onto Lucas's street. It was dusk when they pulled up to his house, but it was completely dark inside and there was no car in the driveway. Lucas started to move from his seat when he noticed a station wagon pull up beside the van and Coach Earl's wife get out. She came to the window and had a quick, quiet talk with Coach Earl. Coach then turned around and motioned to Lucas.

"Come on out here for a minute, Lucas. My wife needs to talk to you."

Lucas went over to the car and leaned in the window. "Lucas, I just talked to your Uncle Roy on the phone."

"Uncle Roy? Why'd you talk to Uncle Roy?" Lucas asked.

"They were trying to find out when you guys were getting back. I need you to get in the car. We need to get to the hospital right away."

Brian Croasmun

CHAPTER THIRTEEN

Lucas followed Coach Earl's wife into the busy waiting area of the emergency room. She disappeared into the crowd, so he stayed near the door as he surveyed the room. He didn't recognize most of the people standing around whispering to one another. He spotted his sisters behind a group. They were seated beside each other but appeared to be leaning in opposite directions on their boyfriends' shoulders. Both had swollen red eyes. Neither sister looked up.

Lucas's breathing was becoming rapid and his stomach was in knots. Coach Earl's wife didn't know any details of what was happening, and now, he didn't know who to ask. His stomach felt worse than it had on any of the rollercoasters. The smell of disinfectant in the room irritated his eyes and nose.

He continued to stand near the door waiting for someone to tell him what was going on. Some of the bodies shifted and an opening to the other side of the waiting area revealed his grandma and Uncle Roy. His grandma pulled a tissue from her brown cardigan sweater and dabbed her eyes and nose. Uncle Roy sat straight up, then shifted to his elbows on his knees, then back up again.

Lucas wandered across the room toward the empty seat beside Uncle Roy. He quietly sat down. Lucas recounted seeing his sisters, Grandma and Uncle Roy, so they were okay. That leaves…his parents. Uncle Roy's head snapped up before Lucas could speak.

"Hey there, champ. When did you get here?"

"What's going on? Why are we here?" asked Lucas. "Did something happen to my mom? Where is she?" His voice rose with each question.

"No, it's not your mom," replied Uncle Roy as he rubbed his jaw with his hand.

"My dad? What's wrong with my dad?" Lucas scooted to the edge of his seat. His eyes widened as he stared at Uncle Roy. His breath came out in short puffs.

"Well, today at work he got to feeling bad, so they brought him here to check him out."

"Who brought him here?"

"Well, they brought him in an ambulance. You see, he kind of passed out and collapsed when he got to feeling so bad, so they called an ambulance."

"Well, they brought him in an ambulance. You see, he kind of passed out and collapsed when he got to feeling so bad, so they called an ambulance."

"He came in an ambulance?" Lucas remembered passing an ambulance on their way home. He was so tired he hadn't raised his head. Lucas squirmed in his seat, then started to rock back and forth. His breaths grew louder and deeper.

"They thought it was best. The guys at the company knew some first aid, so they took good care of him until the ambulance got there. Everybody has done a wonderful job helping him," answered Uncle Roy as he once again shifted in his seat.

"Is he going to be ok?" asked Lucas.

Uncle Roy started to answer, took a deep breath, then let it out slowly through his cheeks.

"So, how was Kennywood? What did you ride?"

"It was terrifying. I hate rollercoasters." Lucas surprised himself with his candidness. He was too scared to hide any emotions now.

"You didn't have any fun?" asked Uncle Roy.

"Yea, I did. I just hate rollercoasters," Lucas replied.

They both fell silent as Lucas sat staring at the floor rocking back and forth in his seat. Uncle Roy shifted in his chair again and a few moments later, shifted more.

By now, it was completely dark outside. There was no television in the room and Lucas couldn't see the clock behind the check-in counter, so he had no idea what time it was or how long they had been here. Minutes? Hours? He was so confused he would have believed whatever anyone told him. He was too tired to try to read a magazine, but not awake enough to make sense of the situation. He knew this much, nobody had come or gone through those doors reading EMERGENCY above them since he had been here, and he still hadn't seen either one of his parents.

Laura walked over to the seat beside Lucas.

"Do you need anything, Lucas? Want me to get you a drink?" she asked. She dabbed a tissue to her eyes and sniffed.

"No, I just want to know how Dad is."

"Maybe they'll tell us something soon." Laura patted him on the back for a second, then returned and sat beside her boyfriend.

Lucas wanted to talk to his mom. He didn't know if he was allowed to walk into the other room or not. He wondered if he should ask Uncle Roy or his sisters where she was. His grandma hadn't raised her head for the past few minutes, so he was afraid to disturb her. He was starting to open his mouth again to say something to Uncle Roy when he was interrupted.

Lucas felt a gentle tap on his left shoulder.

"Heard you had a good ball game this week." It was somebody from Donovan Trucking, but Lucas didn't remember a name or even what he did. He only remembered being introduced before.

"Yeah, I guess so."

"You guess so? I think throwing a one-hitter in a playoff game is pretty impressive."

"You heard about it?"

"I heard all about it. It's all your dad could talk about at work today. He told us all about how he didn't even expect you would pitch at all, and you darn near throw a no-hitter."

"Yeah, that's what happened."

"He was one proud papa. It was so unlike him to stand in the break room the entire day telling and retelling the story to everyone who came in. Well, until he started feeling bad."

"What was wrong with him?" asked Lucas. "Nobody has told me anything other than he felt bad. What happened?"

"I'm not real sure. I was back on the loading docks when the ambulance arrived, so I don't know much about what happened before. I just know we all look up to your dad a lot, and we'll be here to help you guys out as much as we can."

Another mention of the ambulance. Lucas felt guilty thinking his dad might have been in the ambulance they passed. He thought if he would have looked out the window, he might have seen his dad. Maybe he could have told Coach Earl to turn the van around and he could have got to the hospital at the same time and talked to his dad. It might have even been a different ambulance and that wasn't him at all. Lucas rocked harder in his seat.

More people left the waiting area, and some of the standing crowd sat. More time passed when a nurse came through the door, but didn't make eye contact with anyone as she quickly darted through the room and down a hall into the larger part of the hospital. A few moments later the doors opened again, and Lucas's mother slowly walked through. She let the door shut and stood staring ahead. The room went silent. Lucas held his breath.

"He's gone. They did everything they could but couldn't get his heart beating again."

Laura and Linda both jumped out of their seats and into their mother's arms wailing loudly. Grandma turned to Roy and buried her face into his shoulder letting out a muffled sob. Others in the room turned toward one another while some embraced. Lucas sat alone on the edge of his chair unable to move.

His mother raised her head from between his sisters. "Lucas, oh, Lucas," she said as she separated from his sisters and moved toward him. She stretched out both arms and pulled him into an embrace.

She squeezed him hard and began to cry harder and louder than before. Lucas put his arms around her and tried to position his face to breathe.

She held him there for a long time, restarting her crying and squeezing him harder multiple times. After a few moments, she raised her her head but kept her arms tightly around Lucas. Others had begun to approach her, putting their arms around her or both of them, but she never let go of Lucas.

Lucas's tears came slowly and fell on his mom's shoulder. His mind was spinning trying to understand his dad was dead. His dad was just at the playoff game the other day. Just before that, they were passing the Clemente Ball in the front yard. He was still trying to imagine his dad bragging about the one-hitter all day at work. He seemed so real Lucas was having trouble thinking how it was possible he was no longer here.

Lucas still had no concept of time when his mother finally relinquished her hold on him. She continued to keep a hand on his back or shoulder after everyone sat down and began talking quietly. He could tell the adults were in a serious discussion, but he could no longer keep his eyes open. It was a dreamless, fitful, uncomfortable, few minutes of sleep.

"C'mon, honey. Are you awake? Uncle Roy is going to take us home." Lucas's mother gently rubbed his back as he slowly came to life. "You ready?"

Lucas had no idea where the car was or how they would be getting home. Uncle Roy drove a pickup truck, and it wouldn't have enough room for everyone. He released a breath when he saw their station wagon underneath a light post. They'd all fit. He climbed in the backseat, followed by his mother. Grandma sat up front with Uncle Roy. His sisters got in the car with Laura's boyfriend.

"I'll get you guys home, and we'll figure out the whole car situation tomorrow. You'll need to stay home all day anyhow," said Uncle Roy.

They drove by the courthouse on their way home, and Lucas peered up at the clock tower, which showed 2:30 in the dim light. A few minutes later they were home, and everyone shuffled into the living room. Lucas sat down at the end of the couch and leaned back to rest his head, falling asleep immediately.

He woke up to a knock on the door, still in the same spot, with a blanket tucked in neatly around him. When Lucas shifted to see the clock on the mantle, it was almost noon.

Gladys, the sweet old lady across the street, smiled to Laura and handed her a dish of food. She then patted Linda on the arm a couple of times before turning back around and heading across the porch. There were already some deserts on the table, and Laura set the new dish of food down with the others.

Mike's mom came through the door next carrying a meat and cheese tray with a pack of buns. Mike followed. She went into the kitchen where Lucas's mom was, while Mike shuffled over toward Lucas in the living room. Lucas had pulled off the blanket but remained on the couch. Mike stopped by the mantle and grabbed the baseball.

"This it?"

"Yeah." Lucas couldn't muster up much more of a reaction. His body was too tired.

"Pretty cool. I'm still going to come to the championship game when you guys play."

Mike's mother appeared in the living room and quickly shooed him out the door, leaving Lucas alone on the couch. Lucas couldn't fathom playing in a baseball game now.

A few minutes later the doorbell rang, and in came Jessica and her father. Jessica held a stuffed monkey, and her father had something from the local bakery. Jessica walked directly over to Lucas who was standing in the doorway from the kitchen.

"You left this in the van yesterday, and I thought you might want it," Jessica said.

"Nah, it's yours. You won it, so you should keep it."

"I have the purple bear now. This should be yours."

"Why don't you keep them both. I don't know what I'd do with it anyway."

Jessica smiled and gave the monkey a little squeeze. It reminded Lucas even though she was a good second baseman, she still liked stuffed animals, as well.

Lucas could now hear Mr. Snider talking to his mother.

"We wanted you to know how much it meant to us when Dan stood up for Jessica with the baseball league. I know it couldn't have been easy. We didn't want a fight or to cause trouble and he took a lot of the burden I expected to receive upon himself. I will be forever grateful. You know my wife and I are both attorneys. Even though we don't specialize in wills and estates, we might be able to help you if you need any legal advice over the next few weeks. I'm sure there will be things you need to take care of and either one of us would gladly look it over or walk you through anything you need help with. We won't take a penny in return. Your husband and son have made our daughter's life so much easier, it's the least we can do. Here is my card. If I haven't heard from you in a couple weeks, I'll stop by and check how things are going."

He then turned toward Lucas. "That was some game you had the other night. I felt like I was back watching Steve Blass in the World Series. I don't know if they gave out any kind of most valuable player award, but you sure would have won it. I couldn't have been happier for any other kid in the whole league. You know why?"

Once again, Lucas couldn't find the words. He just continued to look at Mr. Snider.

"Without you, Jessica couldn't have been able to play her first season of baseball. She knew some of the stuff other kids and adults were saying, and it hurt her feelings. But every time she came home from a practice or game, she talked about how well you accepted her, and the rest of the team followed your lead."

Jessica was smiling and nodding her head as Lucas looked toward her. He should say or do something here, but he still wasn't sure what. He liked hearing Mr. Snider say all these nice things, but they didn't make him feel any better. He was able to summon the strength to at least get out a few words.

"She wanted to play baseball, and she was good enough to play. I didn't do much."

"The hero is always the humblest. That's why I like you, Lucas. You've got a great son there, Mrs. Billman. Of course, he had a great example in Dan, and I am truly sorry for your loss. I'm serious about letting us help you. You'll be hearing from me soon," Mr. Snider concluded as he waved for Jessica to follow him out the door.

Jessica turned toward Lucas and gave him a hug, squeezing the monkey into his back. Lucas hugged her back hard. They both stood still, pressed against one another. She started to release her arms, but Lucas was still holding on to her. She squeezed him again and neither moved for a few moments more. Lucas finally let go, sniffed hard, and began wiping his eyes with his sleeves.

"See you at the game, Monday," Jessica said. She waved, squeezed the monkey to her chest, and grabbed her father's hand as they walked out the door. Lucas's mom stepped over and put her arms around him as they waved good-bye.

Lucas closed his eyes and took in a deep breath. His father had just died and now there was a championship game on Monday.

CHAPTER FOURTEEN

The funeral was exhausting. Lucas didn't know he had so many relatives in the area, plus he didn't know many of them, either.

The crowd at the dinner following the funeral at the church had dwindled down to a remaining few. Mike's family was one of the last to leave. Mike pushed his chair back under the table as he got up to join them.

"Well, guess I'll see you tomorrow at your championship game," said Mike.

"Um, I don't know if I'm playing or not," replied Lucas.

"Oh," Mike paused and looked at the floor. "Um, alright then, I guess I'll see you sometime." He looked around some more, then left.

Lucas put his elbows on the table and leaned his face on his hands as he folded them together. He turned his head when he felt a hand rubbing his back. He'd been so deep in thought, he hadn't heard the chair pull back beside him.

"Did you get enough to eat, honey?" asked his mom.

"Am I playing in the championship game tomorrow?" asked Lucas.

"I don't know, sweetheart. With everything going on, I hadn't even thought about it." His mom put her hand to her cheek. "I'm not sure what all we'll be doing tomorrow. I just don't know. Do you want to?"

"I don't know. I don't feel like playing. What fun is it going to be now?" He put his face down in his hands.

"I don't know what to tell you, Lucas. Maybe we should just think about it tonight and decide tomorrow. There's no rush." She patted Lucas on the back.

"Never mind, I'm not going to play." Lucas still had his face in his hands.

"If that's what you want, it's fine with me. Everyone will understand."

Lucas was certain that's what he wanted. No game was going to take the place of his dad. What good would it be to play anymore if he didn't have his dad to cheer him on? Who would he pass the Clemente Ball with now? No, there was no reason to play baseball anymore.

The next morning, Lucas was on the couch in the basement watching game shows. He had heard the phone ring a few times already and each time his mom spent a few minutes talking with someone. It rang again, and this time she yelled down to Lucas.

"Lucas, phone call. I think it's Jessica."

Lucas went upstairs and picked up the receiver. "Hello?"

"I just wanted to remind you Coach wants us to come a little early tonight, so we aren't rushed for the championship game. He said fifteen extra minutes would be soon enough."

"I'm not playing tonight," replied Lucas.

"You're not? Oh, I thought you would since, you know, since everything was over yesterday and all."

Lucas could hear nervousness in her voice, and it made him uncomfortable. He wanted her to stop talking so he could hang up the phone.

"Well, I'm just not going to play baseball."

There was a long pause while Lucas listened for a reply. He could hear Jessica breathing, but she wasn't saying anything. He wondered if she was still on the line.

"Are you sure? It might make you feel better. It should be fun. My dad thinks there will be a big crowd because the other teams will want to see who wins after Simpson's Paint Shop got beat."

"I don't care. I don't feel like playing."

"OK, I guess I'll talk to you later sometime. Bye."

"Bye." Lucas hung up the phone and paused a moment.

"Hey, Mom. Jessica wants me to play tonight, but I told her I'm not," said Lucas.

"Is that what you really want to do?" his mom asked.

"I don't know. What should I do? I really wanted to win the championship, but now…" His voice trailed off as he looked toward the ground. "Would you care if I played?"

"Lucas, it's not up to me. I don't mind, but it's your decision. There's no right or wrong answer to this. You do whatever you feel you need to do."

Lucas took a couple breaths and looked directly at his mom.

"What do you think Dad would want me to do?"

A little smile crossed his mom's face. "I can tell you this, your dad loved watching you play baseball. He loved talking about how much you loved to play baseball. If you want to play, he would be fine with it."

Lucas walked into the kitchen and sat down at the table. His mom followed and stood by the kitchen sink. Lucas stared at the table and drummed his fingers lightly while his mom leaned against the counter with her arms crossed. They remained there a few moments in silence before Lucas got up and walked downstairs. He walked across the basement and reached up to the shelf above the television and grabbed the Clemente Ball. He turned it over and over in his fingers, then clasped both hands around the ball. He closed his eyes tight, took a deep breath, then let it out slowly.

He put the ball back on the stand, walked over to the bottom of the basement steps and yelled upward.

"Mom! I'm gonna play tonight!"

Lucas buttoned up his jersey and made sure it was tucked neatly into his pants. His stomach was feeling queasy, but he felt comfortable with his decision. He knew his dad would want him to play, and he wanted to do his best for him.

"Lucas, we'll have to leave in a few minutes," his mom said. "Uncle Roy is going to bring Grandma, and your sisters and their boyfriends are going to come, too. You are going to have quite the little cheering section tonight."

He knew she meant this as a comfort to him, but it only made him more nervous. He was afraid of disappointing all these people if he didn't play well.

Many of the players from both teams were already at the field when Lucas climbed out of the station wagon and headed toward the dugout.

"He's here! Hey, Coach! Lucas made it!" Jessica came bursting out of the dugout. She wrapped her arms around him and squeezed tight. Lucas hugged her back. Lucas didn't care if anyone saw them. He wasn't afraid to let people see how important Jessica had become for him. He would ignore anyone who thought about teasing him, now.

They began to warm up by passing baseball in the outfield before the game. Lucas marveled at the crowd turning into the largest he had ever seen at this field, and the people kept coming. Everyone had multiple friends and family coming to watch them play in addition to the players, coaches, and parents of the teams already eliminated from the playoffs. Lucas even noticed Russ Ledbetter by the outfield scoreboard with his left arm in a cast and a sling. "Ought to be fun for him all summer," mumbled Lucas as he concluded his warm up throws. Lucas's stomach tightened a little bit more.

Coach Earl called the team together. "Jeff, you are going to pitch the first couple of innings, then we'll bring Timmy in the last few innings," he explained.

"What if he has a no-hitter going, Coach," asked Jessica. The whole team burst out in some "Woo hoo!" and "Oh, yeah!" as they smiled over toward Lucas. Assistant Coach Howard patted Lucas on the back. Some of the players were patting Jeff on the back, too. This wasn't as silly of a question as it seemed last week.

"I think we know the plan, now," Coach Earl explained as he winked toward Jessica. "We can't think this will be easy tonight because we beat these guys every game this season. They were all close games, and I've seen how much they've improved. We have to play our best to win."

Coach Earl was, unfortunately, correct in his pregame talk. Conner's Market got hits from three of their first batters and scored the first runs of the game. A bloop hit brought in another run and Donovan Trucking was behind by three when they finally got to bat. Lucas knocked Bobby in for a run, but Conner's Market led 3-1 after one inning.

The second was only a little better. Both teams scored a run, even though Donovan Trucking left the bases loaded. It was 4-2 and things were not going as easily as everyone had planned since Simpson's Paint Shop had been knocked out.

"If we stop them here, we'll be alright. I think we can score lots of runs on them," whispered Jessica to Lucas as they took their positions for the third inning. Lucas nodded his head in agreement, but the knot in his stomach begged to differ.

A bunch of sports clichés were running through Lucas's head as the third inning unraveled. The wheels had come off, the dam had burst, and somebody had left the gate open to the corral.

Conner's Market was getting hit after hit and run after run. Timmy had to be brought in to pitch sooner than planned to try to halt their momentum with only a little success. The inning finally came to an end with Conner's Market adding on five more runs to lead the game 9-2. Donovan Trucking was stunned.

The dugout was as silent as a funeral. The coaches tried to be encouraging, but Donovan Trucking had only been this far behind when they'd played Simpson's Paint Shop and they'd lost all of those games. The tension grew when Jeff struck out by swinging at a ball over his head.

Lucas scanned across the bench and couldn't believe what was happening. The same group who was having the time of their lives on Tuesday evening, cheering on Lucas and his attempt at a no-hitter, were now acting like someone had told them the rest of the summer had been canceled. This isn't why he decided to play today. He had to do something.

He closed his eyes and tried to remember how his dad looked after the last game. He recalled the smile on his face, and how he beamed with pride. That's why he decided to play tonight.

"Why are we all sitting in here pouting like this? We always have so much fun playing baseball, now we're pouting around. Let's at least start making some noise and having some fun. What's it going to hurt? We're already behind by seven runs." The tightness left Lucas's stomach.

"He's right," said Jessica. "We can't sit here and cry about it. Let's toughen up and get back in this game."

Lucas began reflecting back to the day of tryouts and the stir caused by Jessica showing up. He now realized he hadn't thought of Jessica being the first girl to play youth league baseball in their town for quite a while. She was just as much a member of this team as anyone else, and they all had a championship to win.

Timmy must have been listening from the on-deck circle because he stepped up to the plate and ripped the first pitch into the outfield. It rolled to the fence, letting him trot into second base with a double. The next hitter bunted a ball stopping right between the pitcher and third baseman, who stared at each other expecting the other one to pick it up. A walk loaded the bases right before Jessica singled up the middle, driving in two runs. Another single drove in another run before the inning ended on a pop-up. Donovan Trucking had scored three times and made the score 9-5, but more importantly, they'd gotten their energy back. Lucas was more confident than ever.

Timmy got back in his groove on the mound and struck out two of the three batters in the fourth inning. The other hit a sharp grounder that Lucas had to scoop up to his left, then made a strong throw to first base to get the last out. He didn't even notice if his arm was still sore or not.

"Look, their dugout is like ours was a little while ago," noted Jeff. "They act like they're losing, and they're still ahead by four. For now, that is."

"You're right, Jeff. They look scared," replied Lucas.

The team took notice and went into their turn to bat with renewed confidence. A couple of good hits were followed by a couple Conner's Market errors and Donovan Trucking had added two more runs to make the score 9-7. They were still down by two, but no one could tell from their enthusiasm. Every hit and run were cheered, while every out was met with a pat on the back and a word to get them the next time. There were still two innings to play.

The three outs in the top of the fifth came so quickly, Lucas wasn't even sure who had batted for Conner's Market, and he didn't care. He was satisfied they were going in to bat because he thought they could soon be in the lead if things continued as they had the last couple of innings.

Lucas had made the final out on a fly ball during the last inning, so he knew he wouldn't be up for a while. He took a deep breath to relax in the dugout while he watched what his teammates would do. Two walks to the first two batters got the tying run on base. Jessica was the second runner. The next two batters struck out as the momentum shifted from one team to the other. Another walk to Bobby and the bases were loaded.

Lucas was still another batter away from his turn but started thinking he might have a chance to be the hero. He could get to drive in the tying or the lead run. He started warming up in the on-deck circle while Danny stepped in to bat.

Danny hit a short ground ball, and the third baseman charged ahead to field on the run and threw the ball toward home plate instead of first. The throw was so high, it went over the catcher's head and bounced off a pole supporting the backstop. The ball kicked away toward the other dugout. Coach Earl was waving his arms frantically yelling for Jessica to "Go, go, go!"

She ran across home plate with the tying run!

Coach Earl continued to wave for Bobby to run home as the catcher gathered the ball, throwing it to the pitcher covering home plate. Bobby had stopped between bases, but Coach Earl was still yelling, so he took off for home anyway. No one was surprised when the umpire shouted, "You're out!"

"My mistake, guys," Coach Earl yelled toward the team. "I thought Bobby was closer to home plate. I guess I got greedy. Let's go play some defense."

This had now become a one-inning game.

Timmy got the first two batters out before Conner's Market finally showed some signs of life. A couple of singles set them up in great shape to retake the lead with runners on first and second. Donovan Trucking needed a break if they didn't want to fall behind again.

Lucas smoothed the infield dirt with his cleats as he often did, then looked up to see Timmy staring at his fingers. Coach Earl came walking out of the dugout while the rest of the infield met them on the mound.

"My finger's bleeding, Coach," said Timmy.

Coach Earl looked at his hand. "You had a blister that just popped. Happens sometimes to a pitcher. Looks like we're going to have to replace you."

All of the infielders began to look at each other. There was only one pitcher available on this team. Lucas swallowed hard.

"Lucas, how do you feel about taking the mound? The team needs you."

Lucas swallowed hard again. He looked Coach Earl square in the face and forced the air out of his nose. He closed his eyes a moment to recall the picture of his dad's face again. He pulled up his left arm and opened up his glove.

"Give me the ball. I'm ready."

Coach Earl snapped the ball into Lucas's glove. Everyone in the infield smacked him on the back with their gloves before returning to their positions. Timmy went to first base with a fresh Band-aid around his finger.

"We only need one out here, infield," yelled Coach Earl.

"Outfielders get the throw home on a base hit. We can't let the runner from second score," yelled Coach Howard to the outfielders.

The big catcher for Conner's Market was the next player to bat. He hit two hard foul balls making some of their fans ooh and aah.

"Straighten it out, kid," yelled someone from beyond the outfield fence.

He connected on the third pitch and hit a looping fly ball toward short center field. Jessica ran hard toward the ball as Danny came charging in from centerfield. Jessica was never going to get there, but Danny was closing in on the ball now. Danny came to a sudden stop, squinting at the sky. He must have lost the ball in the lights.

The ball caromed down off the side of Danny's head, scraping his ear and bouncing off his shoulder. The ball hung in the air for a moment as it was heading back toward the infield when Jessica reached up instinctively and grabbed it in the pocket of her glove! She turned and held it high into the air to show everyone she had caught the ball. The base umpire was puzzled for a moment as he contemplated the situation.

"She caught it in the air! It never hit the ground!" shouted Lucas as the baserunners continued to run.

The umpire finally raised his right arm in the air and declared, "He's out!"

The coaches for Conner's Market talked with both umpires for a few moments. The home plate umpire did most of the talking as Lucas could tell he was explaining how the ball bounced off Danny and into Jessica's glove and was a legal catch. Lucas watched enough of the bloopers on *This Week in Baseball* on TV to know it was an out. Danny's only injury from the play was a nick on his left ear since it was a glancing blow. The game was heading to the bottom of the last inning, tied 9-9, and Lucas was the first player coming to bat.

"One run is all we need, one run," was repeated by a majority of the players in the dugout.

Yeah, no pressure there.

Lucas grabbed his bat and put on his batting helmet. He took a couple of swings while the pitcher took some warm up throws. He looked around and noticed the crowd. There were people filling all the bleachers, standing along the fences down the foul lines, and also across the length of the outfield. He wondered for a second if there were this many in the stadium the day Clemente got his three-thousandth hit.

It was then he looked at the spot where his dad often stood. It caught his breath for a moment. His eyes focused and there stood Uncle Roy. He looked at Lucas, made a fist, pumped it up and down just a little bit and said, "C'mon, Lucas. I know you can do it."

Lucas felt a surge of energy as he took one more practice swing before heading to bat.

He heard the beating of his heart and nothing else. The first pitch came zooming in as he gripped the bat and swung with all his might. The bat made contact with the ball, but Lucas couldn't feel a thing. The loud "crack" he heard let him know he had hit the ball hard. He could tell the ball was flying toward the outfield, but he wasn't sure exactly where. He dropped the bat and started to run as fast as his feet could carry him.

He had reached first base and saw Coach Howard pointing toward second. Lucas stepped on the corner of the base and made the turn chugging as fast as he could. As he neared second base, the ball was still in the outfield grass. He didn't slow up as he went digging for third. It was at this moment he realized he never saw the signal to keep running from Coach Earl. He was hoping he did the right thing as he pulled into third base, then he saw the ball being caught by the third baseman ten feet away. Lucas was standing on third with a triple. Somehow, Coach Earl didn't mind.

Suddenly, pandemonium broke out in their dugout. Players were jumping up and down, some were shaking the fence on the front of the dugout, while others had climbed up and were pounding on the roof. "We haven't won anything, yet," Lucas whispered to himself.

Lucas's confidence started to soar when he thought about Jeff coming up to bat next. He'd been hitting the ball well lately. Lucas's body started to move as the pitcher began to throw.

Crack! Awwwww. Foul ball. Lucas was almost to home plate when he saw the ball drop outside the foul line.

Lucas caught his breath just in time. Another pitch. CRACK! Everyone jumped to their feet. "Aawwww." Lucas looked up from home plate and watched the ball hook over toward the bushes out of play down the right field line. It wasn't even close to being fair, but Lucas wanted this run so bad he could taste it.

Jeff quickly hit two foul balls getting the dugout excited and each time had Lucas sprinting for home when the balls landed well into foul territory. All of this running had him winded and Lucas was panting hard now. He hoped Coach Earl didn't notice and get the idea of sending in a pinch-runner for him. There was no way he was letting anyone else score the winning run.

For the third time, the pitcher threw the ball, and for the third time, Jeff swung and made contact...This time the ball stayed fair. Jeff had hit a bouncing ground ball toward the shortstop. Lucas didn't wait around and broke for home plate as hard as he could. Everything got quiet as he saw the catcher step in front of home plate and hold up his mitt, ready to receive a throw. Lucas closed his eyes and slid hard across the infield dirt. He crashed into the catcher's left shin guard and everything went black. A crushing weight pinned his body to the ground.

He laid motionless for a moment. He couldn't feel anything but the heaviness holding him down. He couldn't move his arms or his legs. He didn't think he could breathe through his nose or even open his eyes. The only sound he could hear was the ringing inside of his head. A sense of fear began to seize him.

The weight began to release from his chest, but he was still afraid to move. His cheeks filled with air, then burst through his mouth causing a small cloud of dust above his face. The volume of noise from the field started to increase slowly into his ears but was interrupted by the home plate umpire yelling, "Safe!"

Lucas reached up to push the visor of his batting helmet off his face in time to see the entire Donovan Trucking team come racing toward him out of the dugout. One by one, each player dove on top of Lucas at home plate. They rolled around for a minute or two until the pile toppled over revealing filthy Donovan Trucking uniforms and smiles wider than home plate. Donovan Trucking had won the championship!

Lucas couldn't stop smiling as they were presented their first-place trophies and then lined up for a picture. The Sniders snapped picture after picture with their Polaroid camera, passing them out to the other parents. All the moms were waving and blowing on them to dry so the pictures would develop.

Once all the photographers were satisfied, Coach Earl called the team together. "You, too, parents. We want everyone to get in here for this." He waited until everyone had scrunched in together and got quiet before starting to speak. Lucas felt an arm wrap around his shoulders from behind and turned to see his mom.

"This was one of the greatest comebacks I think I've ever seen. You kids never gave up, no matter how far you were down. I was already proud to be your coach, but this game managed to make me even more proud."

The meeting broke up and Lucas received congratulations from everyone in his cheering section. He got hugs from his mom and grandma. His sisters and their boyfriends said they were happy for him, too. Then Uncle Roy stepped in with, "I don't remember teaching you to hit like that, Lucas." He then lifted Lucas's cap and messed up his hair as he laughed.

After returning home, Lucas scrubbed down in the shower while his mom put his uniform directly in the washing machine.

He came into the living room in his pajamas alone, and sat down in the chair, and picked up the trophy from the coffee table. He ran his fingers over the player on the top and felt the marble base. He looked at the gold faceplate with 1973 LEAGUE CHAMPIONS printed on the front. He should be sharing this with his dad.

His shoulders quivered, but he held back any noise. His stomach pulled in sharp bursts. He wiped his eyes with the back of his hand. He leaned back into the chair, lifted his head while more tears came down his cheek as he sat and mourned alone.

CHAPTER FIFTEEN

Summer heat and humidity had Lucas sweating under his sheets. He got out of bed and didn't bother with a light because he knew the way to the bathroom and there would be a little night light on in there. As he left his room, he jumped a little when he saw there was still a light on in the living room, revealing his mom sitting alone.

"Do you need something, honey?" she asked.

"Just getting a drink of water. It's still pretty hot in my room," Lucas answered.

This wasn't the first time his mother had been awake late and sitting alone since his father died. The only sight bothering him more was all the times he watched her sitting at the kitchen table with a pile of papers or looking through the mail and sighing as she read each piece. He had no idea what any of it was, but it obviously was adding to the stress he saw on her face every day.

"Is your fan on? Does it help cool down your room?"

"Yea, it helps. I pulled the covers up and I got too hot, that's all," answered Lucas.

She put on a smile, but Lucas didn't think it was sincere. He had seen her smile before and this wasn't what she looked like.

"Would a cookie help you sleep? I think we have a few left in the kitchen?"

"Nah, I just need some water."

Lucas came into the living room and sat in the recliner by the couch where his mom sat.

"Are you staying up a while, Mom?" he asked.

"I was thinking about heading to bed myself," she answered. "It just gets a little…"

Lonely? Scary? Frightening? Lucas thought to himself. This was how he'd been feeling these past three weeks since losing his dad, but he didn't want to burden his mom. She always cut her sentences lately and never gave Lucas a chance to say how he felt. He didn't know how to get it out either.

"What are you kids doing up so late?" asked Laura in deep fake voice.

Their mom forced a smile. "Can't you sleep either?"

"I was still awake and heard you guys, so I came to see what's happening."

"Why don't you two go back to bed and I'll head in and get some sleep myself," his mom said.

Lucas got his drink of water and went back to bed. He shut the door and climbed back into his bed. He heard Laura's door close, as well. The living room light still shined under his door.

He watched for a few minutes, and then a few minutes more. The longer he saw the light, the more tense his body became. He couldn't relax as long as the light was still on. Slipping out of bed, Lucas moved slowly to his door, and opened it a sliver. Just enough to see his mom still sitting on the couch in the living room, staring at the floor.

His mind wanted to go back into the living room, but he couldn't think of what he would say. He felt his eyes moisten as he continued to see her sitting alone. He was so helpless. He thought about asking her to come to his room, but the words wouldn't come out.

Slowly closing his door, he stepped back into his room wishing he had never stared at the light under the door. He needed help and he didn't know where to get it.

A few days later, Lucas came up from the basement where he was watching TV, which he did most of the day now, and saw his mom sitting at the table, once again with a stack of papers in front of her. She motioned for him to come over.

"Sit down here, Lucas, I want to talk to you for a minute. As you know, your sisters are going to both be leaving in a few weeks, and it's been awful hard to keep up with everything here with them. It's going to be even harder without them. Plus, this big old house is expensive to keep up and with not having your dad's income, well, we are going to move in with your grandmother."

She could have hit him in the gut with a baseball bat, and it would have hurt less. He never thought he'd leave this house, this neighborhood, and everything he knew. Of course, he never imagined his father would pass away, either.

"She's not in the best health anymore, so she could use having someone with her all the time. Uncle Roy stops by, but he's not going to do much cooking or cleaning, and I could be a help to her there. You'll still get your own room and have the same yard your dad had when he was a kid. You'll still go to the same school. I think it will be a different bus than comes here, though. So, you see, it won't be a big of a change for you, will it?"

Won't be a big change? This will change everything!

She examined his face while she forced her smile, but he stared ahead and didn't speak. He squeezed his stomach to hold in his emotions. He could feel it in his throat where he thought he would choke. His body settled down after a few seconds, but he did not share his thoughts.

"We are going to start packing up the house and getting ready for a big yard sale soon, so hopefully we can be ready to move near the start of school. We can use this as a time to get rid of a lot of junk we don't use anymore. Grandma already has a house full of furniture, so we might not need to move too much."

Is this supposed to make me feel better? It should be easy to pack up my life and sell it to strangers?

"Oh, OK." Lucas looked around the room like he was preparing a plan for moving. He was afraid if he saw his mother's face too much he would burst out in a scream or cry. She acted like this was such an obvious solution, he couldn't be the one to ruin it for her.

Lucas left the kitchen and went to his room. He sat on the edge of his bed and put his face in his hands. He couldn't fathom leaving this house, his room, his friends and this neighborhood.

He scanned the room looking over his collection of a lifetime. The thought of packing up his memories and deciding what to keep and what to throw away was excruciating. He couldn't decide where he would begin or if this was going to be easy or difficult.

He couldn't do this now. It was going to have to wait until later. He thought he would go down to the basement to get away from his room and take his mind off this big change for a few minutes.

He looked around at the ping-pong table, the TV, the furniture, and there on the shelf, the Clemente Ball.

He walked over to the ball, picked it up, turned it over in his hand and his stomach became a giant knot. He squeezed his eyes shut and took a long, slow breath in, then out through his puffed-out cheeks. He put the ball back on the stand and shook his head. The basement wasn't making him feel any better.

He retreated back up the steps and out on the porch to sit. Mike saw him, waved from his driveway and started to head over.

"What are you up to?" asked Mike.

Lucas didn't think he could adequately explain how his whole life was being uprooted and he was being forced to leave the only home he had ever known. He was at a loss for the words to tell Mike they would no longer be neighbors and wouldn't see each other very often. He wanted to say this kind of visit was going to be gone, soon.

"Not much," is all Lucas could say. "What are you doing?"

"My mom is making me get some new clothes for my cousin's wedding. We might go out to eat, too, I guess."

"Sounds like fun," Lucas snickered.

"Yea. I better get going before my mom gets mad. I'll catch you later."

This was the kind of thing Lucas was going to miss about Mike. They weren't in the same grade, they didn't play the same sports, and they rarely saw each other outside of their own homes, yet Mike was always there. Their ping-pong games felt epic, even if nobody else ever saw them. He didn't remember Mike's phone number because they almost never called each other. They didn't have to. They would open the door and the other guy would be there. Now Mike was going to be gone, too.

Box after box of their lives had been sold and loaded into strange cars. Lucas stayed out of the way most of the day. They didn't need him much during the sale, so he kept himself occupied with what little he saved for the move. He didn't need much anymore because nothing could replace what he had lost. He planned to quietly hide away this last week before the move.

Lucas hopped on the bus for the first day of school. It was the same bus, the same route, and the same driver until next week.

"I'm moving next week, Homer," said Lucas to the driver. "I'll be on a different bus that goes by my grandma's house."

"Sorry to hear that, man, and sorry to hear about your dad. He always seemed like such a nice guy."

"Thanks, Homer."

The seventh-graders were assembling in front the school to check the posted lists of their new home rooms. Lucas saw Russ moving through the crowd toward him and started to think of what he could say to him. He would have normally prepared some sarcastic response to zing him good, but Lucas couldn't find it in him now. He stood tall and planted his feet to show Russ he was ready to stand up to him.

"Hey, Lucas," Russ said in a regular voice. "Sorry to hear about your dad."

"Um, thanks, man." Who was this strange version of Russ Ledbetter?

"Congratulations on winning the baseball championship. That was a pretty big hit you had. You really smoked that thing."

"Yea, thanks. It was all pretty cool," Lucas answered. He thought it was the right thing to say, even though he didn't feel it inside any longer. It was like a memory of something he had seen on TV that had happened to somebody else.

"Those were pretty cool trophies, too. I think those were nicer than the ones we got last year."

Lucas was feeling awkward having a civil conversation with Russ. He wasn't sure if this had ever happened before.

"Oh, yeah? I didn't see them last year since we didn't win. How's your arm?"

"It's fine. I got the cast off in time to start football practice. Look, it's still skinnier than my other arm." He held up his left arm to let Lucas compare.

Lucas had forgotten all about football. This would have been the first year they could play on a team and he'd missed it. Baseball was always his favorite, but he had planned to give football a try. Lucas couldn't think about the future enough now to know if he would try to play next year. Add it to the list of things he was not doing now.

"Ready to be a seventh-grader yet?" came a voice from behind Lucas. Jessica had snuck up on him.

"Sure, why not?" Lucas answered.

Jessica had come by the house a couple of times lately, and Lucas often made up excuses why he couldn't go places and do things with her. He wished he could tell her how much it meant that she continued to show up and care even though he was too uncomfortable to be social.

"Did you see the sign for the back-to-school dance on Friday? Seventh-graders are allowed to go to dances now. Are you going?" asked Jessica.

"Nope. We're moving on Saturday, so I'd better stay home and help my mom."

"You sure? Students can go as couples now, and I wanted you to come with me. Maybe just for a little while?"

Lucas was torn. He enjoyed being with Jessica, and it was intriguing being able to do things at school for the first time. However, the thought of spending the evening in a crowded gym with the kids from school stressed him out. He wanted to let her down gently. Before he could say anything to her, the bell rang, and the entire grade migrated through the front door into their new school adventures for the year.

Each class brought a new lecture on class rules and what materials would be needed. They passed out textbooks and made book covers to keep them neat. They took papers home to have them signed and brought them back. Lucas didn't mind the mind-numbing pace. He wasn't ready for too much excitement yet. Now, they could get the next task Lucas was dreading over with, too.

There was plenty of room on the big flatbed truck sent from Donovan Trucking and the rest of their stuff fit in Uncle Roy's pickup since they had been bringing over smaller boxes the last few weeks. Lucas unpacked all his belongings and redecorated his new room with all the things from his old one. It looked strikingly similar and much neater. Lucas promised his mom he would keep it this way, but he didn't feel much pressure to keep his promise.

Lucas's mom said he could arrange the basement TV room any way he wanted, since Grandma also had a

TV in her living room. It would be his place to hang out and invite friends. It wasn't as much open space as they had in the old house, but he thought he could make it all fit. The ping-pong table went on one side while there was still room for a couch and chair near the TV on the other. There was also a bookcase he filled up with encyclopedias, leaving the top shelf empty for a couple special items since there was no shelf above the TV.

He looked around after emptying the last box sent to the basement and a sense of nervousness started to tingle in his head. He quickly sprinted up the stairs to find his mom.

"Are there any other boxes left to go in the basement?" asked Lucas briskly.

"I don't think so, honey. Should there be?" answered his mom.

"The Clemente Ball. Where is the box with the Clemente Ball?" answered Lucas a little more forcefully.

"It wasn't in the basement boxes?"

"No, that's why I'm looking up here. What else do we have to unpack?" His jaw was starting to clench.

"I think we have most of it. Maybe there's something in the garage."

He sprinted out the door and found a couple of unopened boxes. One was marked "car wax and rags" and the other "sports equipment." His sisters had labeled all the boxes well, so he knew he had one chance. He opened the "sports equipment" box and saw his baseball glove, his dad's old glove, a deflated basketball, and a Nerf football. His heart was beating so rapidly he thought he could feel it through his chest. He went back into the house.

"Did you find it, honey?" asked his mom. He was struggling to breath properly.

"Maybe your sister knows something. She handled a lot of those boxes. Laura, come in here a minute, would you?"

Laura walked into the room in a dirty t-shirt and ponytail. She had taken on much of the heavy work in preparing for and completing the move.

"Did you happen to remember a box with a couple of old baseballs in it? Lucas can't find them anywhere," asked his mom with concern in her voice.

"I think there were a couple of old baseballs in the box of old sports stuff we sold at the yard sale. Can you believe the guy bought the—"

"YOU SOLD IT?! HOW COULD YOU SELL IT?!" Lucas screamed at the top of his lungs.

Laura looked at their mom with surprise, but her expression couldn't have matched the one on their mom's face. They both stood in stunned silence as Lucas began pacing the floor.

"How could you sell the Clemente Ball? That's wasn't an old piece of sports equipment. That ball was special. Dad caught that ball and Clemente hit it and now they're both *dead*!"

Lucas couldn't stand still, and his mom and sister didn't move.

"Who bought it? Find him and *get it back*!" spat Lucas as he turned toward them.

They both looked at Lucas for a moment, then their mom turned to Laura.

"Do you have any idea who bought it? Maybe we could look him up and give him a call," she said quietly.

"How would I know who he was? I didn't recognize most of the people buying stuff at the yard sale. He said something about using it to entertain his grandkids when they come to visit. He never said who he was or where he lived. All I know is he was fat and bald," answered Laura.

"So now it's gone too, just like everything else. Dad dies and now I have to live in a different neighborhood that isn't close to any of my friends and stay in a room that smells funny!"

"Lucas, I've never heard you—"

"I don't care anymore. I lost my dad, I lost my house, I lost my friends, and now I've lost the Clemente Ball. I don't have anything anymore. All I have is that stupid trophy everyone keeps talking about. I don't care about that stupid thing. Unless it's going to bring Dad back, I don't care about it! Do you hear me?"

Months of frustration had poured out of Lucas and he was now curled up on the end of the couch clutching a pillow with tears streaming down his face. He had tried to remain strong through everything, so far. He couldn't hold it back any longer.

Deep sobs caused him to suck in large amounts of air he couldn't use to fill his lungs. His stomach hurt so bad he thought he was going to throw up. His head pounded, and he couldn't see anything in the room through the water in his eyes.

He could no longer control his body. The sounds, the movements, everything was like someone was moving him like a puppet on a string. He felt his mom's arm go across his back and pull him in, but he continued to heave. His stomach was becoming sore from the convulsions.

His breathing started to slow down, and he was starting to hear sound in the room again. His mom was rocking him back and forth while tears poured down her cheeks. His sisters had both sat down and joined in the crying.

Lucas felt better letting all of the pressure go. He still didn't feel right. It was a relief to finally show how he had been feeling inside and allow his emotions to surface. However, his situation was still the same. His dad was gone, and his best memory was gone with him.

Brian Croasmun

CHAPTER SIXTEEN

The next week of school became a hum-drum routine for Lucas. He went to school, came straight home, watched TV, ate dinner, did his homework, watched more TV, and went to bed. He simply didn't feel like doing anything else.

He was walking through the kitchen when he noticed Jessica riding her bike up the driveway Saturday morning. She didn't bother him anymore about the dance after the first day of school and Lucas had avoided everyone most of this past week. He did confide in her about losing the Clemente Ball. It was a short conversation and the only one he had with another student all week.

"What do you want?" asked Lucas semi-politely, as he opened the screen door only far enough to put his whole head through.

"I came by to see you. I might even have a surprise for you. Are you going to ask me to come in or not?" Jessica replied.

He pushed open the screen door enough to allow her to pass. She carried a brown paper grocery bag.

"You missed a fun dance last week. I think the entire seventh-grade was there." Jessica was looking at

Lucas's face, and paused. Lucas didn't reply. "There was lots of music and decorations and some terrible snacks. That was the only bad part."

"Maybe next time," he mumbled back.

"I suppose you want to know why I am here, so I'll get to it. I know you have been upset since you lost your Clemente Ball, so I think I might have something to help," she began. Jessica then unrolled the top of the paper bag she had brought and started to reach inside. She pulled out a clear plastic box containing a sparkly white baseball with writing on it. She stretched out her arm offering the box to Lucas.

Lucas took the box and slowly brought it up in front of his face. He turned the box over revealing the writing on the ball saying, "Feliz Navidad, Roberto Clemente." He raised his eyebrows as he examined the box closely. He held it for a few moments more, then his breathing started to speed up. He took a slow deep breath before attempting to speak, but no words came.

"It's my dad's Clemente Ball. Once I told him what happened to yours, he asked me to offer you his Clemente Ball in its place. See, it's signed by him and everything. I know it's not the same thing, but this one is probably better. I think it might be worth some money. I was never allowed to touch it before I put it in this paper bag. It's something, isn't it? I knew it would cheer you up," she concluded.

He stared straight at her and his lip began to quiver. His breathing became slow and steady.

Jessica's smile spread across her face. She scooted to the edge of her chair.

His eyes moistened as he finally found the words. "I don't want it."

Jessica's smile immediately disappeared, and her eyebrows began to furrow. A puzzled look appeared on her face.

Once again, his breathing was coming rapidly. He repeatedly clenched his fists, then released them. He tried closing his eyes and breathing out of his nose. His emotions were once again too much to hold in. He clenched his teeth as he began to speak.

"You don't understand. I want the ball my dad caught. I want the ball I threw with my dad before the playoffs. That is the only ball I want. I don't care who signed it," answered Lucas forcefully.

He handed the box back to Jessica. She reached out slowly, then quietly put it back in the paper bag and rolled up the top. She continued to stare at him as she picked up the bag and put it on her lap.

"I'm only trying to help, Lucas."

"If you want to help me, figure who the guy was that bought my ball and bring it back. Until then, there's nothing anyone can do." Lucas put one fist into his other hand and squeezed.

"I guess I'll be going back home, then," Jessica whispered. Her face was tense, and her eyes were becoming glassy.

"Yea, I guess," answered Lucas.

She looked at him again. Her mouth opened a little, but she didn't speak. She swallowed hard before shaking her head back and forth. She let out a breath and got up from her seat. She went straight through the door without speaking. Lucas shut the door behind her and went to the basement to be alone.

He sat down on the end of the couch, put his face in his hands and quietly sobbed, hoping no one followed him down.

Lucas took another lap around the TV channels trying to find something to watch and settled on the local evening news. He stared at the screen without listening to what the news anchors were saying. He mainly watched the pictures of firetrucks, hospitals or school buildings.

"Hey, honey, could you come up and help Uncle Roy for a little bit?"

"What's he doing?" asked Lucas as he came up the stairs.

"He's going to work on the mower. Remember, it keeps shaking so hard when you get it started. He says it's probably a spark plug, or an air filter, or a couple of other things I can't remember. He brought some parts from the store, so he thinks he can fix it with a little help," she explained.

Lucas didn't know how he was going to be much help to Uncle Roy. He didn't think he could be much help to anyone right now, especially doing something he didn't know how to do. He had been mowing the last couple of years and the mower had been running fine, so he was never around when his dad had to work on it.

He did feel he owed his mom a favor or two. He knew he had been moping around this past week. He also knew his mom had been extra nice to him trying to improve his spirits. He felt he owed her this much.

His body felt sluggish coming up the stairs. He was starting to notice his lack of movement and how it was affecting his body. Hopefully, he wouldn't need to do any heavy lifting.

Uncle Roy was still wearing his shirt from the auto parts store where he worked. One benefit of having him as a relative was being able to call him and say what part was needed. He would bring it home with him and probably help fix it, too. He was never in a big hurry to go home since he lived alone. Throw in a free meal, and he might not leave.

"Let's get to work there, young buck. We've got to get this fixed, so someone can get the yard mowed again before fall," joked Uncle Roy from the kitchen.

"You mean so I can mow the yard," Lucas said as he rolled his eyes.

"Glad to see you volunteered."

They went out to the front of the garage and pulled out the lawn mower. Uncle Roy fiddled around in a bag and pulled out a new spark plug.

"Let's try this first. Give me the wrench, and we'll see if we can get the old one out."

A couple of grunts, a few hard turns, and Uncle Roy was holding the old spark plug in his hand.

"Look at this, Lucas. No wonder the mower ran so rough. This tip is all charred up. Hand me the new one."

Lucas handed him the new spark plug, and Uncle Roy had it back in place in no time.

Brian Croasmun

"Now give a couple tugs on the rope and see if she starts," Uncle Roy ordered.

On the second pull, the motor roared to life and the engine hummed. Uncle Roy poked here and there, then shut it off.

"Runs like a dream, now, wouldn't you say? It always works out great when the first thing you try fixes the problem. Now you can get the yard mowed this weekend."

Uncle Roy put his toolbox into the back of his truck and pushed the mower back into the garage. He winked at Lucas and said, "I think I saw some brownies inside."

They retreated into the house together. Uncle Roy walked over to the coffee pot and poured himself a cup, then joined Grandma and Lucas's mother at the kitchen table. Lucas went into the living room and turned on the TV before plopping himself down on the couch. The conversation could be heard from the kitchen, so Lucas paused before turning up the volume.

"I honestly don't know what else to do for him. It seems like nothing can make him happy, and he has no interest in doing anything but watch TV. I know it's probably been the hardest for him, and I don't want to upset him anymore. I would do anything if I thought it would help," explained Lucas's mom.

"He's the saddest boy I've ever seen," said Grandma. "I can usually cheer him up with pancakes, but he just gobbles down a stack and heads right back to the TV."

Lucas didn't respond to what he was hearing, since he thought they believed he couldn't hear them. He had tried to remain strong for everyone, then lost control of himself, and now he felt like he'd lost hope. He knew he'd given everyone extra stress by his behavior, but he didn't know how to feel better now. Everything in his life was gone, and he had no idea how to get anything back.

"Think about this. Where did you ever see that kid the happiest?" asked Uncle Roy. "When he was out there playing baseball. I've watched him do other school activities and hanging out with his friends before, but I never saw the twinkle in his eye like I saw this year. And I don't mean just the championship stuff. You could see every game he was out there at shortstop, he thought nothing could go wrong. He was proud, confident, and a great leader. We've got to somehow get him involved with baseball again."

"Any idea how to do that?" asked Mom. "Maybe take him to a Pirates' game?"

"Season is over this weekend and they are on the road," answered Uncle Roy. "How about I try again to get him outside and at least pass the ball with me?"

Baseball. Lucas had detached any emotion from the game ever since they got back from Kennywood and he went racing to the hospital. He wanted to get that feeling back, but it was too much without his dad. He ached to feel that way again.

"It might work if you can do it without mentioning the Clemente Ball," Mom answered.

"She's right," Lucas mumbled to himself.

Lucas was trying to make up his mind if he was better off to go outside and pass ball to get it over with so they would all leave him alone or keep telling them he wasn't interested. He didn't want to be seen out in the front yard crying and everyone trying to make him stop.

"I've got an idea how to get him out there," offered Uncle Roy. "We can't ignore Dan, so I'll tell him about me throwing ball with his dad when we were kids. Maybe it will be like a transition to get out there and throw with me."

"Give it a try," answered Mom, "It's as good as any idea we've come up with."

Hearing Uncle Roy's plan gave Lucas a warm feeling inside. He decided to give Uncle Roy a chance.

"Hey Lucas," yelled Uncle Roy as he entered the living room. "Did I ever tell you about your dad trying to teach me how to throw a curveball when we were kids?"

"He taught you? He was teaching me, but I was only able to do it twice," answered Lucas. "Once when I was trying to show Jessica."

"Of course, got to show it off for the ladies." Uncle Roy laughed.

Lucas just stared. "The other time—"

"Let me guess," interrupted Uncle Roy, "the playoff game."

"Yep, the next-to-last batter. Everyone was bummed about them getting the hit, so I thought I'd see what would happen, and I threw a pretty good one."

"Struck that kid out, if I remember right." Uncle Roy smiled.

Lucas chuckled inside. Uncle Roy was always talking during a game and would often miss details. It was probably a lucky guess.

"What do you say to you and me heading out to see if you can do it now?" Uncle Roy asked.

He thought Uncle Roy might want to talk baseball more than he wanted to play it. He pictured his dad passing baseball with Uncle Roy when they were kids, then moved ahead to his dad passing with him. Maybe passing with Uncle Roy wouldn't be so bad. Lucas was tired of being so sad.

"I think I know where the stuff is, but I don't know if we have a baseball or not."

Saying that statement hurt a little.

"Our stuff should be out in the garage." Lucas went through the door into the garage first and went to the box labeled "sports equipment." He pulled out his glove first, then paused as he reached in to grab his dad's glove. He swallowed hard, then pulled the glove out.

Uncle Roy glanced around the garage, then headed for the only other box in the building marked "car wax and rags".

"That's all car stuff, Uncle Roy. You won't find any baseballs in there."

"Then what's this thing?" Uncle Roy had reached in and pulled out a dirty baseball and held it up for Lucas while he kept digging.

Lucas froze. He wasn't even sure he was breathing. He was staring at the baseball and afraid to move. He was afraid to get any closer to it. He was afraid of what it might be, and he was afraid of what it might not be. He continued staring while his heart beat harder and harder in his chest. Uncle Roy unknowingly continued to dig.

Lucas had to take a closer look. His body would not cooperate. He decided to reach out and grab it, yet his arms stayed at his sides. Every time his mind chose to move closer to the ball, his body would counteract and keep him still. Uncle Roy was still digging.

"What's this thing?" Uncle Roy pulled his other arm slowly out of the box and tried to reach it over his head while holding on to the ball and box with the other. Lucas couldn't tell what he was talking about and didn't possess the ability to move, either.

Uncle Roy let the box drop loudly to the floor, but none of its contents spilled out. He then turned around toward Lucas and held up a square, brown piece of wood with a large hole in the middle.

Both of Lucas's eyes welled up immediately. He squeezed them shut for a moment and tears squirted out and down his cheeks. He squeezed them closed again with the same result. Cautiously, he stood up and reached for the baseball. Uncle Roy handed it to him with a puzzled expression. He turned it over in his hands, then pulled it up to his face to take a closer look, pausing every few inches. He had to turn the ball again to examine it properly, but plainly in dirty letters it said, "National League Baseball."

Lucas reached out his free hand and waved, as if to ask for the wooden stand. Uncle Roy handed it to Lucas with the same puzzled expression as before. He placed the baseball into the large hole of the wood and gave it a wiggle to make sure it wouldn't roll away. He stepped back awkwardly and seated himself on top of an old bucket. His body began to heave heavily as he appeared near the point of collapse.

"Hey look, there's another one in here." Uncle Roy flipped this one out of the box and Lucas snatched it with one hand. He then pulled both balls into his chest, closed his eyes for a minute while his smile grew, then opened them to look at the three adults standing with him in the garage.

"We had it with us the whole time," said Lucas.

Brian Croasmun

CHAPTER SEVENTEEN

Early Sunday afternoon Lucas walked in to the phone and grabbed the receiver.

"Who are you calling, honey," asked his mom.

"Oh, I thought I might call and see if someone would want to come over," answered Lucas.

"Somebody I know?" his mom asked.

"Uh, yeah. Somebody that's been to our old house lots of times."

His mom smiled. "It will be nice to see Mike again."

Lucas chuckled, then started to dial.

"Hey, whatcha doin'?" Lucas asked.

"Not much. Why? You got something exciting to do?"

"I was just thinking you might want to come over and do something, you know, like we did back at my old house." Lucas paused to listen and looked over his shoulder for a second.

"Sure. I can leave right now."

"Why don't you bring your baseball glove, too." Lucas hung up the phone and went straight to his room.

A few minutes later there was a knock on the door. Lucas was already coming out of his room and went to answer it with a smile.

"Come on in."

He opened the door wide and Jessica stepped through the door carrying her baseball glove. Lucas had his baseball glove on his hand.

"We're going out to the yard for a while," Lucas announced to nobody in particular. His mom and grandma smiled to each other as they watched them exit the front door.

They went out to the yard and Lucas opened up his glove to reveal a baseball to Jessica.

"Wait. Is that it?" she asked.

"Yep."

"You're sure about this?"

"I'm sure."

Jessica reached her hand up to cover her mouth and nose as she blinked her glistening eyes. "I'm really touched that you invited me over for this. I mean it."

"I couldn't think of anyone else I would call."

"So, we're going to pass with the Clemente Ball."

"Yep." He tossed the ball lightly into the air before letting it fall into his glove. "We're going to pass with the Clemente Ball."

The top shelf on the bookcase in the basement now has two dirty baseballs with a shiny trophy displayed between them and Lucas has an even more wicked curveball.

ABOUT THE AUTHOR

 Brian Croasmun began his teaching career in 1989 as a special education teacher at New Martinsville School. Three years later, he began teaching reading to 7th and 8th graders, and has been there since. During his teaching career he has coached baseball, football, basketball, softball and soccer. In 2001, he filled in on a high school broadcast on local radio and has continued calling football, basketball, baseball and softball.

Brian has a degree in elementary education, a master's degree in curriculum and instruction, and is a graduate of the Institute of Children's Literature.

The Clemente Ball is his first novel.

FOLLOW THE AUTHOR ONLINE

 Brian Croasmun, Author

 @briancroasmun

 @briancroasmun

www.briancroasmun.com

briancroasmun@gmail.com

44016893R00105

Made in the USA
Lexington, KY
05 July 2019